TO THE VAMPIRES AND THE GHOULS, ALL IS ARTIFICE . . .

A young, healthy blanked body is worth several million credits. You can buy a copy of your own mind tapes for less than a hundred credits—if you have any use for it, that is.
—*I. F. + S. C. Operation Logbook,* Appendix III

★ ★ ★

Austin Worms, chief somatician, submitted that the body had a most unusual character and history.

It was agreed that the lack of information about the final condition of the Ismael Forth body was unfortunate and suspicious. Culpable negligence was only one possibility.

Candy Darling remarked that the original Ismael Forth Body, if undamaged, would fetch top credit on the zombie market.

—I. F. + S. C. Operation Logbook

"One of the brightest new talents to come along in years."

—Robert Sheckley
Fiction Editor
OMNI

Beyond Rejection

JUSTIN LEIBER

A Del Rey Book

BALLANTINE BOOKS • NEW YORK

The author thanks the trustees of the estate of Dylan Thomas for permission to quote the line "After the first death there is no other."

A Del Rey Book
Published by Ballantine Books

 Published in the United States by Ballantine Books, a division of Random House, Inc., New York, and simultaneously in Canada by Random House of Canada, Limited, Toronto, Canada.

Library of Congress Catalog Card Number: 80-66166

ISBN 0-345-29054-2

Printed in Canada

First Edition: September 1980

Cover art by Martin Hoffman

Acknowledgments

The author thanks the following for writing space, inspiration, and/or criticism: Diane Bairstow, Steve Branson, Chris Ciesiel, Carol Maddox, Stanley Martens, Massachusetts Institute of Technology, Douglas Miller, Alice Phalen, and his PHI 136 class, Fall 1979. Deeper debts are owed Marion, Martha, Fritz, and, of course, Shasta IV of the University of Houston, cougar.

Contents

I.	The Body Had a Most Unusual Character	1
II.	Why They Are Called Vampires	11
III.	Fine-Tuning	17
IV.	Negligence Was One Possibility	25
V.	Basic Physical Procedures	31
VI.	Psychological Rejection	39
VII.	A Young, Healthy Blanked Body	49
VIII.	Top Credit on the Zombie Market	55
IX.	Motivation Is Crucial	65
X.	A Prehensile Tail	73
XI.	They Must Play	81
XII.	Learning to Be a Woman	87
XIII.	The Masks of Gender	97
XIV.	Philpritz Modulation	111
XV.	The Older Harmonizers Whisper	117
XVI.	Learning to Love	125
XVII.	Self and the Other	145
XVIII.	Taking Over the Controls	151
XIX.	The Most Intimate Bodily Relationship	159
XX.	Beyond Rejection	173

Beyond Rejection

I

Austin Worms, chief somatician, submitted that the body had a most unusual character and history.

—I. F. + S. C. Operation Logbook

Gxxhdt.

Etaoin shrdlu. Mmm.

Anti-M.

Away mooncow Taddy-fair fine. Fine again, take. Away, along, alas, alung the orbit-run, from swerve of space to wormhole wiggle, brings us. Start now. Wake.

So hear I am now coming out of nothing like Eros out of Death, knowing only that I was Ismael Forth—stately, muscled well—taping in, and knowing that I don't know when I'm waking or where, or where-in. And hoping that it is a dream. But it isn't. Oh, no, it isn't. With that goggling piece of munster cheese oumphowing on my earlids.

And seemingly up through endless levels and configurations that had no words and now no memories. Wake.

Austin Worms, interning somatician, sighed. He slipped a bookmark into Bruhler's *The Central Equations of the Abstract Theory of Mind* and stretched the back muscles that concentration and frustration had kinked. He had the basic theory of the human mind. As any high-schooler knew from reading the pioneering twentieth-century work of Alan Turing and Noam Chomsky, the human mind could be described quite apart from the physical brain. Similarly, one could describe the software, or program, of a computer without talking about the particular kind of electrical circuitry which realized it. But Worms was cowed by the nonstandard number theory in which the software of the human mind had to be given. Since he had set himself the task at the beginning of his internship at Rockefeller, he must have pushed himself into Bruhler's equations a hundred times. He found his grasp of the abstractions beginning to cloud up before he got through the preliminaries. He would probably still be hitting the book when he finished his career. God help us ghouls, he thought.

At the center of the laboratory to which Worms' study cubicle was annexed, a human female body jogged atop a rubber-surfaced treadmill. A gradual accumulation of minor variations had led the body from the center track of the treadmill. The slight change in the *slap-slap* of the jogger's feet alerted Worms. Before the warning lights began to flicker on his board he took position behind the jogger, slapped one thigh in a practiced way that would have the running figure back on center in a hundred paces without oscillation or straying to the other side, and adjusted some of the wires that led into the helmet that the jogger wore. He paused only to stare once again at the unusual physical endowment of the body's backside. Whoever got this one was in for some surprise. Still, the face had fine, firm lines. The small breasts bounced.

His intercom buzzed.

"Hey, Ghoulie, you got company. Just some Regional Representatives aides and guests. Nothing fancy—they're not anything to do with funding reviews, just a bit of sightseeing. We'll be up in five, right?"

"Okay. And don't call me by that name, Terry."

Austin Worms sighed again. There would be five to

ten people milling about his lab for an hour or so, knocking things over, fiddling with knobs, or at least looking like they wanted to fiddle with knobs, asking silly questions, and cracking the usual jokes about zombies and what somaticians *did* with zombies when no one else was around. At least they wouldn't say "Hey, Ghoulie" to his face.

Terry, the snotty, gangling kid who was tour guide, would want to come back and jaw after passing the tour group on through the psychetician lab down the hall. And the vampire business didn't take more than fifteen minutes to fade into absolute boredom for anyone who didn't love mathematics, so Terry would be back soon. Worms put Bruhler back onto the bookshelf and sighed again. He would have denied that it was a sigh of relief.

Humming a space-marine tune, he drew a canister of coffee beans from his hiding place at the back of the hormone refrigerator. He sent a measure of beans through a fungal micromincer that cost as much as a personal helicopter. The lab was fresh with the odor of perfect coffee when Terry and his gang of six entered. The jogger jogged on. He would let her run on for the aides to see. Sugar level would need a slight adjustment and the rest just a visual check and a feel of the musculature. A good somatician could tell a tiny deviation in a blood chemistry level as a good harmonizer could "hear" a discord between some tape bits and the blanked brain's latencies, though the somatician couldn't say exactly what it was about the feel or look of the zombie that indicated the deviation.

He and Terry had finally got one of the guests, a lean young beauty, to stop prancing about and settle down next to the aide who brought him. Worms began his spiel: "People often think that it ought to be simple enough to just *manufacture* an adult human body, like building a house or a helicopter. You'd think that, well, we know what chemicals are involved, and how they go together, how they form cells according to DNA templates, and how the cells form organ systems regulated by chemical messengers, hormones, and the like. So we ought to be able to build a fully functional human body right up from scratch."

Worms moved so that he blocked their view of the jogger. He brought his drained coffee cup down for emphasis.

"And, of course, we could build a human body up from scratch, theoretically, anyhow. But no one ever has. In fact, no one has ever even started to. De Reinzie manufactured the first fully functional human cell—muscle tissue—in the middle of the last century, about 2062 or so. And shortly after that the major varieties were cooked up. And even then it wasn't really manufactured from scratch. De Reinzie, like all the rest, built some basic DNA templates from actual carbon, oxygen, hydrogen, and so on, or rather from simple sugars and alcohols. *But then he grew the rest from these.* That's growth, not manufacture. And nobody's come closer to building an organ than a lab that made a millimeter of stomach wall for several million credits a couple of decades ago.

"I don't want to bother you with the mathematics," he continued, looking away from Terry. "But my old professor at Tech used to estimate that it would take all the scientific and manufacturing talent of Earth and the rest of the Federation something like fifty years and a googol credits to build a single human hand.

"You can imagine what it would take to make something like that," he said, moving out of their line of vision and gesturing at the jogging figure. He took the clipboard that hung next to the treadmill's controls and scanned the sheets on it.

"This body had been blank for three years. It has a running-time age of thirty-one years, though of course Sally Cadmus—that's the person involved—was born over thirty-four years ago. What with demand, of course, three years is a long time for a body to remain out of action. She's in good health, fine musculature for a spacer—says Sally was an asteroid miner here. Seems the body spent two years frozen in a Holmann orbit. We've had it for four months and we're prepping it now. You might see her walking around any day now.

"But Sally Cadmus won't. Her last tape was just the obligatory one made on reaching majority and she left no instructions for implantation. I trust, people, that all your tapes are updated." He gave them the family doctor look and went on, moving closer and dropping his voice.

"I have my mind taped every six months, just to be safe. After all, the tape is *you*—your individual software, or program, including memory store. Everything that makes you *you*." He walked up to the aide who had brought the beautiful young man.

"You—for instance—Ms. Pedersen, when did you have your last tape job?"

The aide, a gaunt red-haired woman in her mid-thirties, snatched her arm from around her young man and glared at Austin Worms.

"What business—"

"Oh, I wouldn't really expect you to say in front of other people." He grinned at the others as Pedersen subsided. "But that's the whole point, you see. Maybe she has been renewing her tape yearly, which is what our profession recommends as an absolute minimum. But a lot of people neglect this elementary precaution because they are so appalled by the thought of severe bodily injury. They just let things slide. And because the topic is so personal, no one knows, no one asks, no one reminds them until the once-in-half-a-million accident happens—truly irreparable body damage or total destruction.

"And then you find that the person hasn't taped for twenty years. Which means . . ."

He surveyed the group to let it sink in. Then he saw the beautiful girl-child. Terry had been hiding her, no doubt. A classic blond-haired, blue-eyed girl in her midteens. She was looking straight into his eyes. Or *through* them. Something . . . He went on.

"Which means if he or she is lucky and there's estate money, you've got someone who has to face all the ordinary problems of rejection that come in trying to match a young mind with what is almost certain to be a middle-aged body. But also the implant has all those problems multiplied by another. The implant has to deal with a world that is *twenty years in the future*. And a 'career' that is meaningless because he lacks the memory and skills that his old mind picked up over that twenty years.

"More likely, you'll get the real blowout. You'll get massive rejection, psychosis and premature essential senility, and death. Real, final mind death."

"But you would still have the person's tape, their software, as you call it," said Ms. Pedersen. "Couldn't you just try again, with another blank body?" She still had her hands off her young man.

"Two problems. First"—he stuck his index finger in the air—"you got to realize how very difficult it is for a mind and a body to make a match, even with all the help us somaticians and psycheticians can provide, the best that modern biopsychological engineering can put together. Even with a really creative harmonizer to get in there and make the structure jell. Being reborn is very hard work indeed.

"And the failure rate under ordinary circumstances —tapes up-to-date, good stable mind, decent recipient body—is about twenty percent. And we know that it jumps to ninety-five percent if there's a second time around. It's nearly that bad the first time if you got someone whose tapes are twenty years out of date. The person may get through the first few days all right but he can't pull himself into reality. Everything he knows was lost twenty years ago. No friends, no career, everything out of shape. Then the mind will reject its new body just as it rejects the new world it has woken up to. So you don't have much of a chance. Unless, of course, you're the rare nympher or still rarer leaper.

"Second, the Government underwrites the cost of the first implantation. Of course, they don't pay for a fancy body—a nympher body, that is. You'd pay more than two millions credits for one of those beauties. You get what's available and you are lucky if you get it within a year or two. What the Government underwrites is the basic operation and tuning job. That alone costs one and a half million or so. Enough to pay my salary for a hundred years. Enough to send the half-dozen or so of you on the Cunard Line Uranium Jubilee All-Planets Tour in first class."

Austin had been moving over to the treadmill control console while speaking. As he finished, his audience noticed a large structure descending from the ceiling just over the jogging figure, Sally Cadmus' body. It looked like a cross between the upper half of a large mummy and a comfortably stuffed armchair. Austin glided over to the treadmill. The audience watched the structure open like an ancient iron maiden. Some noticed that the jogging figure was slowing down.

Austin arrived just in time to complete a flurry of adjustments on the jogger's control package before the structure folded itself around. Two practiced blows on the back of the jogger's thighs brought the legs out of contact with the slowing treadmill.

"It's a lucky thing that implantation is so risky and the sort of accident that calls for it so rare," he said as the structure ascended behind him. "Otherwise, the Kellog-Murphy Law, which underwrites the first implantation, would bankrupt the Government."

"Where is the body going?" asked the blond-haired youngster. Austin could see now that she was probably no more than ten or eleven years old. Something about her posture had made him think she was older.

"Normally it would go into a kind of artificial hibernation—low temperature and vital activity. But this body will be implanted tomorrow, so we'll keep it at a normal level of biological function." He had given the body an additional four cc.'s of glucose–saline plasma beyond the program. That was to compensate for the extra jogging. He hadn't done the official calculations. It wasn't that such mathematics was more than a minor chore. If you had asked him to explain, he would have said that the official calculation would have called for half again as much plasma. But he sensed that the body got more than usual from every cc. of water, from every molecule of sugar. Perhaps it was something in the sweat smell, the color and feel of the skin, the resilience of the musculature. But Austin knew.

The somatic aides would have said that Austin Worms was the best ghoul in the Solar System, a zombie's best friend. And they would have meant what they said even if they went on to joke.

Austin had vomited for the first and only time in his life when he learned the origin of the slang terms "ghoul" and "vampire."

The sounds of Terry's tour group faded as they moved up the hall to the psychetician laboratory. But Austin did not return to Bruhler's *The Central Equations of the Abstract Theory of Mind*. He had been puzzled by what the eleven-year-old blond girl had said to him before sauntering off to catch up with the rest of the tour. She had said, "I bet that mind is gonna be in for a real shock when it wakes up with that thing on its backside." He wondered how she could know that it wasn't just part of the crazy-quilt system of tubes and wires that the jogger had on her back.

"I'm Candy Darling," she had added as she left the room. Now he knew who she was. You never knew what to expect in a harmonizer.

II

> Psycheticians take care of minds. That's why they are sometimes called vampires. Somaticians are called ghouls because they take care of bodies.
>
> —I. F. + S. C. Operation Logbook, Append. II, Press Releases

Germaine Means grinned wolfishly at them. "I am a psychetician. What Terry would call a vampire. Call me Germaine if that does not appeal."

They were seated facing a blackboard at one end of a large room which was otherwise filled with data cabinets, office cubicles, and computer consoles. The woman who addressed them wore severe and plain overalls. When she had first come to the Norbert Wiener Research Hospital—NWRH—the director had suggested that the chief psychetician might dress more suitably. That director had retired early.

"As you know from what Austin Worms told you, we think of the individual human mind as an abstract pattern of memory, skill, and experience that has been impressed on the physical hardware of the brain. Think of it this way: when you get a computer factory-fresh, it is like a blanked human brain. The computer has no subroutines, just as the brain has no skills. The computer has no data arrays to call on, just as the blanked brain has no memories.

"What we do here is try to implant the pattern of memory, skill, and experience that is all that is left of a person into a blanked brain. It is not easy because brains are not manufactured. You have to grow them. And a unique personality has to be part of this growth and development. So each brain is different. So no software mind fits any hardware brain perfectly. Except the brain that it grew up with.

"For instance," Germaine Means continued, softening her tone so she would not alert Ms. Pedersen's boyfriend, who was dozing in a well-padded chair, his elegant legs thrust straight out in full display, tights to sandals. "For instance, when pressure is applied to this person's foot, his brain knows how to interpret the nervous impulses from his foot." She suited her action to her words.

"His yelp indicates that his brain recognizes that considerable pressure has been applied to the toes of his left foot. If, however, we implanted another mind, it would not interpret the nervous impulses correctly —it might feel the impulses as a stomachache."

The young man was on his feet, bristling. He moved toward Germaine, who had turned away to pick up what looked like a pair of goggles with some mirrors and gears on top. As he reached her, she turned to face him and pushed the goggles into his hands.

"Yes, thank you for volunteering. Put them on." Not knowing what else to do, he did.

"I want you to look at that blond-haired girl who just sat down over there." She held his arm lightly as he turned and his balance wavered. He appeared to be looking through the goggles at a point several degrees to the right of Candy Darling.

"Now I want you to point at her with your right hand—quick!" The young man's arm shot out, the finger also pointing several degrees to the right of the girl. He began moving his finger to the left, but Germaine pulled his hand down to his side, outside the field of vision that the goggles allowed him.

"Try it again, quick," she said. This time the finger

was not as far off. On the fifth try his finger pointed directly to Candy Darling, though he continued to look to her right.

"Now off with the goggles. Look at her again. Point quick!" Germaine grabbed his hand the instant he pointed. Though he was not looking directly at Candy Darling, he was pointing several degrees *to the left* of her. He looked baffled.

Germaine Means chalked a head and goggles on the blackboard, seen as if you were looking down at them from the ceiling. She drew another head to the left of the line of sight of the goggled head and chalked "15°" in to indicate the angle.

"What happened is a simple example of tuning. The prisms in the goggles bend the light so that when his eyes told him he was looking straight at her, his eyes were in fact pointed fifteen degrees to her right. The muscles and nerves of his hand were tuned to point where his eyes were actually pointed—so he pointed fifteen degrees to the right.

"But then his eyes saw his hand going off to the right, so he began to compensate. In a couple of minutes—five tries—his motor coordination compensates so that he points to where his eyes tell him she is—he adjusted to pointing fifteen degrees *to the left* from usual. When I took the goggles off, his arm was still tuned to compensate, so he pointed off to the left until he readjusted."

She picked up the goggles. "Now, a human can adjust to that distortion in a few minutes. But I could calibrate these so that they would turn the whole room upside down. If you then walked around and tried to do things, you would find it difficult. Very difficult. But if you kept the goggles on, the whole room would turn right side up after a day or two. Everything would seem normal because your system would have retuned itself.

"What do you think will happen if you then take the goggles off?"

Candy Darling giggled. Ms. Pedersen said, "Oh, I see. Your mind would have adjusted to turning the, ah, messages from your eyes upside down, so when you took the goggles off—"

"Precisely," said Germaine, "everything would look upside down to you until you readjusted to having the goggles off—and it happens the same way. You stumble around for a day or so and then everything snaps right side up again. And the stumbling-around part is important. If you are confined to a chair with your head fixed in position, your mind and body can't tune themselves.

"Now I want you to imagine what happens when we implant a mind into a blanked brain. *Almost everything will be out of tune.* The messages from your eyes won't simply be inverted, they'll be scrambled in countless ways. Same thing with your ears, nose, tongue—and with the whole nerve net covering your body. And that's just incoming messages. Your mind will have even more problems when it tries to tell the body to do something. Your mind will try to get your lips to say 'water,' and Sol knows what sound will come out.

"And what's worse is that whatever sound does come out, your new ears won't be able to give your mind an accurate version of it."

Germaine smiled at them and glanced at her watch. Terry stood up.

"Terry will be wanting to take you on. Let me wrap this up by saying that it is a very simple thing to play someone's mind tape into a prepared brain. The great problem is in getting the rearranged brain, the cerebral cortex, speaking strictly, to be tuned into the rest of the system. As Austin Worms may have told you, we start an implant operation tomorrow. The initial tape-in will take less than an hour. But the tuning will take days and days. Even months, if you count all the therapy. Questions?"

"Just one," said Ms. Pedersen. "I can understand how difficult it is for a mind to survive implantation. And, of course, I know it is illegal to implant a mind that is over eighty-five. But couldn't a person—if you call a mind a person—live forever by passing through body after body?"

"Okay, that's a tough one to explain even if we had a lot of time and you knew a lot of mathematics. Until this century it was believed that senility was a byproduct of the physical breakdown of the body. Today we know that a human mind can have roughly one hundred years of experiences before it reaches essential senility, however young the body it occupies. As you know, a few successful leapers have survived implantation after a fifty-year wait. So a leaper might, in theory, still be functioning a thousand years from now. But such an individual's mind will not be able to encompass any more lived experience than you. When all there is of you is a tape in storage, you aren't really alive."

After they had filed out, Germaine Means noticed that the blond-haired girl had remained.

"Hi, I'm Candy Darling," she cried. "I hope you don't mind. I thought it would be fun to sneak in on the standard tour. Get the smell of the place."

"Where's your VAT?"

III

Harmonizing calls more for dramatic than scientific talent. A harmonizer fine-tunes body and mind through a combination of sensitivity and imagination.
—I. F. + S. C. Operation Logbook, Append. II, Press Releases

François Vase's gaunt frame, encased in black silk pajamas and an antique robe, was stretched out upon a genuine nineteenth-century Chesterfield sofa that he had purchased from the Boston Museum of Fine Arts. Candles fitfully illuminated walls covered with the drawings of Aubrey Beardsley and S. Clay Wilson. Both artists whose elegant and black decadence reminded Vase of two of his favorite historical milieus. One the gas-lit London of Jack the Ripper. The other the San Francisco of the 1960s and 1970s before the Great Repression that swept North America in the last decade of the twentieth century (a bizarre union of opponents of pollution and technology, abortion, drugs, feminism, intellectuals, and sexuality that repealed the original Bill of Rights, deported or killed over a million people, and faded out after a decade, leaving North America only too willing to ratify the Concordat of Tokyo).

François was in his midsixties, but a taste for ancient forms of self-abuse and a disdain for the more cosmetic capacities of modern medicine made him look much older. He was reading Anton de Bruyier's *Lewis Carroll and Pre-Twenty-first Century Deca-*

dence, a work that had once made it fashionable to believe that Carroll's chief talent was as a photographer of prepubescent nude girls. An observer might have thought that the room appeared smoky because of the candles and the clay pipe that François sucked at intervals. The pipe held tobacco rather than the more usual mixtures of marijuana and Vegan leaf that those who smoked, smoked—and in private. And the tobacco was one of the rare traditional strains that still contained carcinogenic tars.

The observer would have been wrong about the smoky appearance of the room, though. Concealed ventilators cleaned the air, while a projector system that could put a hologrammic ballet performance on the table next to the sofa carried out the humble function of creating the visual illusion of smoke and augmenting the candlelight. While François had a taste for traditional vices, he took some precautions. He had his lungs washed at regular intervals.

A set of vibrations projected in François Vase's inner ear reminded him that it was 5:00 P.M. He stretched his six-and-a-half-foot body, shivering delicately, and opened the teakwood box on the table, where he had put aside his pipe. The box was lined with worn green velvet and had variously shaped depressions for its contents in the manner of a case for draftsperson's instruments or an orchestral flute. The five depressions held two squat bottles, a leather strap, a set of needles, and a hypodermic syringe, whose shining brass barrel bore the inscription BAYERISCHE MEDIZINALWERKZEUGEN 1905. François swabbed his arm with fluid from the bottle labeled ALKOHOL—the fluid, in fact, was a much more modern disinfectant—and injected himself with a carefully measured amount from the bottle labeled DIACETYLMORPHINE.

With practiced efficiency his long fingers replaced the strap from his arm to the box, sterile-closured the needle, and refilled the velvet depressions. He settled back with time to spare, ready to give his full attention to the first stirrings of the red flush that would soon wash over him. He found a peculiar nostalgia in the ancient drug—a nostalgia that was more pain than delight. You could say that a modern drug-user would look on his habit as a drinker of Vegan malt Scotch might regard someone who drank moonshine whose mash was softened by battery acid. After the development of the orthoamines at the end of the twentieth century, opiate and barbiturate addiction disappeared completely, just as corn-silk smoking had ceased centuries earlier when farm boys were allowed tobacco.

The voice in François Vase's inner ear said, "Priority-two call, sir, on your private line. Germaine Means."

"Entry. Sound only. Hello, Germaine. I have an early flick laid on. I'll be with you at the VAT room by ten o'clock tomorrow morning. What's up?"

"Afraid to display your depravities, you old hermit? Let me in."

A projection of Germaine Means stood before him.

"Germaine," he said, "I like to savor a rush."

"You've had your heroin? I'm just checking around with the whole crew. Odd. Many of them have quirky little rituals that they go through before an implant begins. One of my psycheticians does four hours of mantras the night before. If you want to have a runny nose when we start, who am I to complain? Harmonizers are strange people."

"Bosh, Germaine. It gives me a good feeling of sensitivity if I start an implant with a mild withdrawal reaction. I always want to harmonize this mind and that body—that's my job—but the reaction gives me a special grip on things. I feel the incoherences. There is . . . look, the director agrees, Worms agrees, indeed *you* agree—"

"François, calm down. I really am *not* complaining. I wanted to make sure you took your shot on schedule.

Candy Darling has turned up. Been on Earth since yesterday. The whole staff is ready." She broke off to look at the drawings on the walls.

"You do have peculiarly revolting tastes, François."

"I have a need of extremes, Ms. Means. It will be quite interesting to harmonize with a nympher. I've always thought the nymphing experience would benefit a harmonizer. I would have done it myself were the failure rate not so great. The desire must drive one so . . ."

Both the material François Vase and the ghostly Germaine Means were silent.

The nympher will face the struggle of implantation and a ten-percent risk of failure because the nympher so wants the experience of living once more through to puberty. The experience of living from infancy to fourteen or so, with reinforcement taping through the first few years. And most of the small number of successful nymphers prefer to sell out at fourteen and start again, though many will bring up their body to sixteen or seventeen in order to get a better price. Germaine brought the silence to a close.

"Enough, enough, François. Now let me review. The Sally Cadmus cortex has a point-seven-five on the Lashley Scale, Losey alpha-one-three-three-six. The Ismael Forth mind has a point-oh-oh-five compatibility on the Broca-Shannon inequalities. We're going for Antagonistic-Null Tracking Measures all the way through."

"Index?"

"Close. Look." A ghostly blackboard appeared behind Germaine's projection. It began to fill with figures.

Back at the NWRH, some five hundred miles to the south, Austin Means raised his arm in a ritual toast along with his fourteen somatician assistants. They were now alone in the sky-top staff lounge. Candy

Darling and Germaine Means' two associate psycheticians had left to relax at the frizzies.

"Vampires are uptight
They're sticklers for rules
Zombies are all right
But three cheers for the ghouls!"

Though the somaticians hit the last line hard, that quality of boisterousness was not enough to disturb the sky-top bartender. Somaticians were ghouls, after all.

The bartender was, however, finally moved to expel the rump of the somaticians when they chanted an ancient nineteenth-century verse—a verse celebrating the career of two men of Edinburgh who found simple murder a more convenient method of supplying medical cadavers than mere grave robbing.

"Up the close an' doun the stair,
But an' ben wi' Burke and Hare.
Burke's the butcher, Hare's the thief,
Knox the boy that buys the beef."

The bartender was not so much bothered by the noise. He thought that the second line in particular must be a reprehensible reference to sodomy. Austin Worms could have told him that he was wrong about that. *But* and *ben* were Scottish for the squalid kitchen and bedroom in which Burke and Hare, and their common-law wives, smothered fifteen people. When he bought the bodies, Robert Knox, head of the Edinburgh College of Surgeons, was on of the most notable anatomical lecturers in Europe. François Vase had once bid at a private antique auction for one of the inch squares of tanned flesh from Burke's body, promptly flayed after execution by some enterprising Scotsman. He had intended it as a macabre gift for

Austin Worms. Fortunately the bidding went too high.

In fact Austin had left the party before the advent of Burke and Hare. Feeling mildly tipsy and sentimental, and very secretive, he was floors below in the body-storage area. Moving noiselessly, he had locked all the entrances to the somatician laboratory complex. Now he tripped the switches that would return the Sally Cadmus body to the center of the somatician lab.

Five minutes later, if you had entered the lab, you would have seen a man and woman dancing. Dancing a slow and wholly chaste Vegan pavane. Austin led his partner with infinite and wistful respect. A touch here, a gentle pull there, with hardly any use of the maze of controls on her back. It was a kind of goodbye. And tomorrow would be a kind of death too.

In fact someone had entered the lab, and as silently as Austin Worms. Germaine Means watched them from the darkest corner of the lab, near Austin's study cubicle. She was not a sentimental person but she was not a fool. She watched as the dance ended and Austin kissed Sally Cadmus gently on the cheek and looked a final time into those sightless eyes. Germaine knew that Austin would have calculated the effect of this midnight tryst on the blanked body to the nth degree. It would not interfere with tomorrow's operation.

Austin Worms had been caring for the Sally Cadmus body for months. He knew it in a way that no lover ever knows the body of his beloved. Knew its graceful harmonies and taut reflexes, its subtle concordances of gut and circulation, of skin and lymph. Tomorrow an alien structure would be etched into this brain and all would be changed, all subtly transfigured in a way that few but Austin would notice or care about. This was a very private mourning. Austin stood, head bowed, for a time after the body shuttle had returned Sally Cadmus to storage.

Germaine Means came up behind him but she did not touch him until his head had straightened. "Come on, Austin," she whispered as she put her arm around his shoulder. "We have a very full schedule tomorrow. Let's call it a day."

She marveled at the fact that she had whispered.

IV

It was agreed that the lack of information about the final condition of the Ismael Forth body was unfortunate and suspicious. Culpable negligence was only one possibility.

—I. F. + S. C. Operation Logbook

At 5:02 A.M. the sunlight hit the communications mast of the Norbert Wiener Research Hospital in Greater Houston. The rays came most directly through the air over New Orleans. Before earth-heaving became part of systematic agriculture, the rays would have come minutes earlier and from a more southerly direction.

Floors below, the Sally Cadmus body was receiving a spectrum of chemicals. Chemicals that would build muscle tone and resilience, fortify vascular resistance to extreme pressure fluctuation, and generally prepare tissue and organ systems for the insult and trauma of implantation: ergonovines, orthoamines, acetylfluoridates. The body was already carefully enmeshed in the implantation chamber of the VAT operating theatre. Four scrubbers, under the direction of the body somatician team, had just finished smoothing the body in. A few millimeters of rumple might cause an ugly thrombosis. Inside the transparent cylinder the body could move limb, torso, head, or the tiniest segment of face tissue in free response to any muscular activity. Equally, the incredible net of sensor-transducers that registered such activity could itself produce any pressure or movement that the control consoles directed.

At 5:30 A.M. Germaine Means' Vegan Siamese was playing the black-panther-stalks-the-white-hunter game atop the bookcase next to Germaine's bed. Vegan Siamese are a protected and registered subrational ET catkind, general intelligence of a chimpanzee, specialized hundred-word language capacity, and a peculiar sensitivity to romance and politics. They name themselves. This creature called himself Koullah, possibly as this allowed the pleasing alliteration of "Koullah kill."

Koullah had acquired a taste for the campy *Tarzan and the Round Table* films. He could pick up only a word here and there. Of course he had no sense of the campiness. Koullah would play through the panther-stalk segments over and over while Germaine and Tommie were out. And sometimes when they were asleep, with the sound low. Having attained his present post with a mock stealthiness that sent shivering flashes from his flaring nostril to his hindquarters, which were now squirming up behind him, Koullah looked down on the helpless white hunter, muttering softly, "Oh, vhite perzonz, Koullah ksill."

Unfortunately, Vegan Siamese are not nearly as coordinated as more ordinary cats. They require a disproportionately large skull to house a cerebral cortex with three times the volume and six times the folding of the ordinary cat brain. Koullah's romantic temperament overbalanced caution. He fell with a screech of claws and a warning cry on the sleepers below. Germaine decided to get up. As she finished her cup of coffee in the kitchen bay, Koullah slumped abjectly in a corner, still calling out, "Zootly, zootly, Koullah sbad."

Today was the day. It was only partly to break off Koullah's mournful exploitation of *The Three Mullamulgars* that she called on him for a big-day-and-good-luck. She left the apartment near the climax of an enthusiastic chant that sounded like repetitions of "Sgermaine zot chizen sgood." Koullah was an unspeakably expensive present from a multibillionaire nympher implant, and Germaine was delighted that he should employ metaphor in the fashion of the chimpanzee Washoe, the first recognized subrational. In Koullah's value system, "eating chicken" meant ultimate effort and grand success.

At 7:00 A.M. Austin Worms and his somaticians began their checklist, working from Austin's central body console through the six specialized ones—eyes, ears, body, face, nose, and tongue, in their working language. They would be finished by nine o'clock. Time for coffee and a bite before the 10:00 A.M. countdown. Austin planned for a little rest and good sugar-protein levels for starters. He hadn't slept well.

At 7:15 A.M. François Vase settled into his seat on the Boulder-Houston flick. Candy Darling felt a delicious shiver run through her as she looked at her body in the fresher mirror in the L.B.J. Houston Hotel. She had worked over the Ismael Forth mind file until three o'clock, but she felt like she'd had a full night's sleep.

At 8:15 A.M. the wall separating Austin Worms' somatician laboratory from the still larger VAT complex folded upward into the ceiling. Germaine Means could see her whole crew milling about. *Good chicken eating,* she said to herself. The two body somaticians had to call on Austin Worms to muster enough authority to get François Vase and Candy Darling to stop chattering so they could start smooth-in.

Germaine coughed them to order at 10:00 A.M., March 27, 2112 A.D.

"Sally Cadmus–Ismael Forth implantation. Body, thirty-one years' running time. Dorsal bioprosthesis. Mind, twenty-six essential years on tape. Chief psychetician, Germaine Means. Chief somatician, Austin Worms. We have harmonizer François Vase as the double and harmonizer Candy Darling as the other."

Germaine stood at the controlling console, flanked by her two seated associates. The implantation chamber was directly behind her. The two similar chambers containing François Vase and Candy Darling were to her right. She faced the somatician consoles, which curved like a kidney from Austin Worms' master console, a few feet to her left, through the various sensory panels to the general body console some fifty feet down the operating theatre. As always, she thought of the consoles as a rough representation of the real proportions of the human neurological systems. The "eyes" and "ears" formed the nearest two of the sixths of the kidney. Then came "face"—that meant facial recognition, gestures, expressions, and so on. The "tongue," which covered speech abilities, formed the middle of the kidney with the "nose" board—actually, smell, taste, part of balance and sexuality. The "body" console, whose concern was the body from the neck down, was the center of attention for the first hour of implantation. The first thing an untuned mind might do is to halt the circulatory system or to order the entire musculature to tear itself to pieces. Gross physical adjustment came first. Sense tuning came later.

Austin would immediately direct a professional staff of fourteen through the day, with general directions and an occasional countermand from Germaine Means. But by tomorrow he would be the only somatician left on the team of six that would carry through the rest of the implantation. Austin had his master control console set to replicate the body console's display as the taped-in countdown was completed.

François Vase, who could tune his chamber so that his body would experience everything that happened to the Sally Cadmus body or could reverse matters so that the implant "double" would duplicate all that he did, had cut all his circuits to the implant chamber. Vase waited to see the implant body writhe and flail about like an extreme case of Saint Vitus' dance. His work would begin as they started to tune the senses. Candy Darling would have little to do until the next day.

Tuning worked from the bottom up but with frequent backsteps. The hormone-organ system has a distant and rough relationship to the mind—though there are psychosomatic stomach ulcers and low-blood-sugar depressions. Austin Worms had the system wide open right from the initial tape-in. Later he would fine-tune the system by asking François Vase to get himself piping up a scale from apprehensive to wildly frightened, while Worms calibrated the blood pressure and adrenal levels to run in unison. Of course Austin would be asking a François Vase who would be so connected with the Sally–Ismael complex that what he felt, she felt. The muscular–nervous system of the body was the first big step, then the senses and sense coordination—and back to the motor system, and so on and so on.

Through the long day a cacophony of messages—in sound, in electricity—circulated through the room. Few would make immediate sense to the ordinary person, many made sense only to two or three of the people in the room . . .

"Austin, ear and tongue. We cannot have that solution for plosive feature recognition. Squishy. You have to add a neurological lattice. We're checking catastrophe and main-sequence theoretic. Don't go cheap. We want her to hear right down to Brownian noise." The system formed by the eyes and ten-gram brain of a bald eagle had forty times the acuity of human vision. But a good human ear could not be made more sensitive without running into the static of random molecular motion . . .

"Austin, I want to feel happy and active. Pipe up by ones at three-minute intervals."

"Germaine?"

"Okay. But stop at four."

This short interchange would have to be understood in context. François did not ask Austin to stimulate his own body. The harmonizer had to manage his (or her) own body chemistry by pure imagination. The implant complex got the drugs. And François' lips did not produce the François-sounding voice. Had François moved his lips so, at that point the implant would have duplicated his lip movements. François' voice was initiated by a delicate, typewriting-like movement of his fingers that worked through a computer to produce a reasonable facsimile of François' speech . . .

"Antagonistic-Null Tracking Measure."

"Bend her right leg, François. . ."

"Retinal Quadrant Three down-in and counting . . ."

"Nose locked and out . . ."

"How do you hear that, Candy? . . ."

"I only look that way. I'm ten years older than François, damn it . . ."

"We got eyes! We got eyes! . . ."

". . . and leaping like a ballerina . . ."

"Cool and clean. Go."

V

Austin Worms declared that basic physical meshing procedures were complete.
—I. F. + S. C. Operation Logbook

Gxxhdt.

Etaoin shrdlu. Mmm.

Anti-M.

Away mooncow Taddy-fair fine. Fine again, take. Away, along, alas, alung the orbit-run, from swerve of space to wormhole wiggle, brings us. Start now. Wake.

So hear I am now coming out of nothing like Eros out of Death, knowing only that I was Ismael Forth—stately, muscled well—taping-in, and knowing that I don't know when I'm waking or where, or where-in. And hoping that it is a dream. But it isn't. Oh, no, it isn't. With that goggling piece of munster cheese oumphowing on my eyelids.

And seemingly up through endless levels and configurations that had no words and now no memories. Wake.

"Helow, I'm Candy Darlinz."

"I am Ismael returned" was what I started to try to reply. After the third attempt it came out better. And the munster cheese had become a blond-haired young girl with piercing blue eyes.

"Your primary implantation was finished yesterday, finally. Everyone thinks you're a success. Your body is a pip. You're in the Norbert Wiener Research Hospital in Houston. You have two estates clear through probate. Your friend Peter Strawson has covered your affairs. It's the first week of April, 2112. You're alive."

She stood up and touched my hand.

"You start therapy tomorrow. Now sleep."

I was already drifting off by the time she had closed the door behind her. I couldn't even get myself worked up by what I was noticing. My nipples felt as big as grapes. I went out as I worked my way down past the belly button.

The next day I discovered that I had not only lost a penis. I had gained a meter-long prehensile tail. It was hate at first sense.

I had worked my way up to consciousness in slow stages. I had endless flight dreams—walking, running, staggering on, away from some nameless horror. And brief flashes of sexuality that featured performances by my (former) body.

I really liked my old body. One of my biggest problems, as Dr. Germaine Means was soon to tell me. I could picture clearly how it had looked in the mirrors as I did my stretch and tone work. Just a hair over six foot four. Two hundred and five pounds, well-defined muscles, and just enough fat to be comfortable. A mat of curly red chest hair that made it easy to decide to have my facial hair wiped permanently. It felt good to be a confident and even slightly clumsy giant, looking down on a world of little people.

Oh, I wasn't a real body builder or anything like that. Just enough exercise to look good—and attractive. I hadn't in fact been all that good at physical sports. But I had liked my body. It was also a help in the public relations work that I did for IBO.

I was still lying on my back. I felt shrunk. Shrunk.

As the warm, muzzy flush of sleep faded, my right hand moved up over my ribs. Ribs. They were thin and they stuck out, as if the skin were sprayed over the bare cage. I felt like a skeleton until I got to the lumps. Bags. Growths. Sacks. Even then part of me realized that they were not at all large for a woman, while most of me felt that they were as big as cantaloupes.

You may have imagined it as a kind of erotic dream. There you are in the hospital bed. You reach and there they are. Apt to the hands, the hardening nipples nestled between index and middle fingers. (Doubtless some men have felt this warm reverie with their hands on real flesh. The women may have felt pinch and itch rather than the imagined sensual flush. I know whereof I speak. I now know a lot of sexuality is like that. Perhaps heterosexuality continues as well as it does because of ignorance: each partner is free to invent the feelings of the other.)

But I was quite unable to feel erotic about my new acquisitions. Both ways. My fingers, as I felt them, felt pathology. Two dead cancerous mounds. And from the inside—so to speak—I felt that my flesh had swollen. The sheet made the nipples feel raw. A strange feeling of separation, as if the breast were disconnected, nerveless jelly—and then two points of sensitivity some inches in front of my chest. Dead spots. Rejection. I learned a lot about these.

As my hand moved down I was prepared for the swerve of hip. I couldn't feel a penis and I did not expect to find one. I did not call it "gash." Though that term is found occasionally in space-marine slang and often among the small number of male homosexuals of the extreme S&M type (Secretary & Master). I first learned the term a few days later from Dr. Means. She said that traditional male-male pornography revealed typical male illusions about female bodies: a "rich source of information about body-image pathologies." She was certainly right in pointing out that "gash" was how I felt about it. At first.

I was not only scrawny, I was almost hairless. I felt *really* naked, naked and defenseless as a baby. Though my skin was several shades less fair—and I passed a scar. I was almost relieved to feel the curly groin hair. Gone. Sticklike legs. But I *did* feel something between my thighs. And knees. And ankles, by Sol.

At first I thought it was some sort of tube to take my body wastes. But as I felt down between my legs I could tell that it wasn't covering those areas. It was attached at the end of my spine—or rather it had become the end of my spine, stretching down to my feet. It was my flesh. I didn't quite intend it—at that point I can't say that I intended anything, I was so shook—but the damned thing flipped up from the bottom of the bed like a snake, throwing the sheet over my face.

I screamed my head off.

"Cut it off" was what I said after they had given me enough betaorthoamine to stop me flailing about. I said this several times to Dr. Germaine Means, who had directed the rest of them out of the room.

"Look, Sally—I'll call you that until you select a name yourself—we are not going to cut your tail off. By our calculations such a move would make terminal rejection almost certain. You would die. Several thousand nerves connect your brain with your prehensile tail. A sizable portion of your brain monitors and directs your tail—that part of your brain needs exercise and integration like any other component. We taped the pattern of your mind into your present brain. They *have to* learn to live together or you get rejection. In brief, you will die."

Dr. Means continued to read me the riot act. I would have to learn to love my new body—she practically gushed with praise for it—my new sex, my new tail. I would have to do a lot of exercise and tests. And I would have to talk to a lot of people about how I felt. And I should feel pleased as pisque to have an extra hand.

My new body broke into a cold sweat when I realized that I had—truly—no choice. I wasn't poor, assuming what I had heard yesterday was true. But I certainly couldn't afford an implant, let alone a desirable body. What I had, of course, came free under the Kellog-Murphy Bill.

After a while she left. I stared at the wall numbly. A nurse brought a tray with scrambled eggs and toast. I ignored both nurse and tray. The thin-lipped mouth salivated. Let it suffer.

By midday I was sure that I was feeling bladder pressure. By the time Candy Darling showed up there was pain. The betaorthoamine had long ago worn off. I itched. My hunger had given way to nausea. I wanted to die or at least sleep. But this scrawny, cancer-lumped thing was demanding more and more attention.

"I hear you've been nasty," said Candy Darling. She took up a seat next to the bed. The armchair was low and the bed high. She leaned forward, elbows with two blue eyes goggling between were inches from my face. She kissed me. Small hands felt my face. There was a smell which I might call a cross between baby powder and playground. There was a playful nip on my cheek. And then, suddenly, she was sitting on my midsection, beaming down at me.

For a few seconds I had felt like some monstrous mannequin in a mad doll house. But this was thrown aside by a storm of sexual feeling coupled with tears. I simply cannot explain how I felt.

"Now let's have a look at you," Candy broke in, pulling down the sheet and yanking open the top of my gown. My reaction was instinctive. I tried to cover the breasts. But Candy had enough leverage to hold my hands aside.

"Nice boobies," she said. "Yours stick straight forward. I'll have some in a year or two. And I'll get hair and periods and all that."

I now felt the pressure of her buttocks on my belly excruciatingly.

"I have to use the toilet."

"What'll you give me, huh?" She squirmed, which made my problems worse.

"Please get off me." I felt weak and nervous.

"Okay, but you got to promise to be my slave for the rest of the day—promise?"

I promised.

She took my arm as I got up, but I shook her off. And then nearly ran into the wall as I lost my balance. I looked down at the toilet bowl and realized that I would never aim down at it while standing again.

"Hey, you got a real bush," said that sparkling voice. I slammed the door on it. I urinated but this did not seem to relieve all of the pressure. I got up too quickly and became very sick indeed. It now appeared fortunate that I had not eaten breakfast. As I finished my dry heaves I felt those cool and capable hands again. She led me back to the bed.

"Gee whiz, what does it feel like, huh?"

A menstrual period was all I needed.

It was not, however, all I got. Candy demanded my hours of slavery with all the unreason of a golden eleven-year-old. I was only to learn that Candy Darling was an eighty-year-old spy a few days later.

Actually, the slavery game was good for me in a way. Candy got me walking around and seeing people. She toured me through the VAT—Vital Activity Transducer. It was the operating theatre where the (my) implant was done. I wore a loose coverall and hid the tail by running it down one leg. I had a confrontation with Candy over this last. She wanted me to leave it bare—"Looks wild, like a freeble's lutch" —curving it up behind me like a squirrel's tail. As if it were a flag!

The next days were full of tests and interviews. They were so full that some of the details are fuzzy. I didn't understand much of it. I had slumped from outrage into a stolid depression.

Candy Darling was a relief from this. We continued the game, which cast me as a slightly dumb big sister. I knew, of course, that it was a game. On the third day I told her as much. Her reaction landed me in a completely new situation.

VI

Psychological rejection would be the real issue from now on.

—I. F. + S. C. Operation Logbook

Of course, I sensed from the first that Candy had to be more than an innocent bystander. She knew too much and—let's face it—I was not the sort of person to attract such patience and help. Besides, she could stand up to Dr. Germaine Means, a feat which would have added to the laurels of a double Nobelist with the stature of a Lincoln and the muscles of a gorilla. One thing that made me painfully aware of Candy's role was the name question.

Obviously, I had to have a name. From the start they followed Dr. Means' line; they called me Sally. I could see the point, of course. They wanted me to accept the scrawny female body. I ran into the same three-point litany in every therapy session I had those first three days. One, "A mind has no sexual identity." Two, "You will really come to love it—just lean back and let your body give you a ride." Three, "Think of how lucky you are to be able to experience both sexes' sexuality." What they didn't say said it all: Love it or lose it.

I collided with a scrubber from another floor the third morning. As we disentangled, his hand cupped a buttock briefly. He gave a little wink and twist of his hips as he sauntered away. That time I did vomit. The incident brought the name matter to a head. After I cleaned myself up I set off to tell Dr. Means. Perhaps it was an accident that Candy was there in Dr. Means' laboratory too. Want to bet?

I had the matter worked out in my own mind. Obviously, I should retain Forth as my last name. Common enough practice for implants. And I had all sorts of memories of my parents, though they were the Procyon wormhole away and naturally I hadn't seen them in the three years since they emigrated. I certainly had no memories of Sally Cadmus' parents.

And, being reasonable, I would have to concede that I couldn't go on being *Ismael* Forth. Though an implant could inherit the estates of both mind and body, the implant was a new legal entity. So why not a nice name like *Patricia?* Even Dr. Means couldn't criticize a bona fide female name like that, right? Wrong.

Not that I got to lay out my whole position. When I got to the name Patricia, Dr. Means laughed loudly and abruptly, and convulsively. So loudly and so abruptly that Austin Worms, my body therapist, and some tall old guy looked in from next door to check on what was happening. But they just stood there, the other side of a sizable laboratory, so they could not hear what Dr. Means went on to say. Which, I suppose, is just as well. *Embarrassment* was the word for what was going on with me. *Embarrassment* may seem a petty word, but what it names can be some of the most self-destructive and unmanning experiences one can go through. Perhaps Dr. Means spoke quietly out of some consideration for my state. But *what* she had to say certainly didn't seem intended to make me feel any less embarrassed.

"Look, Forth, you are so unbelievably transparent, you are so damned dumb, you make me want to laugh, cry, or just hug you. No threat intended by that last part—I will not touch you.

"Forth, you are trying to name your fate. You are like some guy who claims to want a gentle, sensitive, and nonviolent son and insists on naming the boy Spike. Except that you are doing a job on yourself. You know as well as I do that 'Patricia' normally shortens to good old 'Pat.' You are not expecting to be called 'Patty,' are you, Patty dear?"

I had to admit that that horrible possibility had not occurred to me. The way she hit the *t*'s in *pat-tee* (not *paddy*) irked me. She wasn't finished.

"Look, I would not mind, indeed I would be more than happy, if you were seeing your way to being a *woman*—a *woman*, got it?—a *woman* who happened to like putting on some classical male moves. You would be fine as a woman who liked to be called Pat. But that is not what is going on with you. You, or rather a twisted-up part of you, insists that it is still a male and that he will be a female *only over his dead body*."

Though I was getting angry, hurt, or whatever, I don't know that I would have been able to say anything back. In my case my guardian angel Candy stepped in.

"Germaine, if Forth wants to be Patricia Forth, that's her right." Candy had been leaning against a desk a few feet from the table where Dr. Means and I were sitting. Now she stood between Dr. Means and me. She wore a pullover and white exercise shorts. Her legs glowed. I had no idea whether her tan was melanohormones or overexposure to sunlight.

"Of course I know Forth has the legal right. In any case the proper way to avoid rejection is to get the implant to make choices, to coordinate, come alive. But I have to point out consequences." Germaine stood up as she said this.

"Germaine, you are so committed to simple truths."

Candy pulled my ear lobe in a friendly but infuriating way.

"Patricia here has a name which might become Pat, gee whiz!, and so you conclude that she's trying to hold on to a male identity. *Un*healthy. Should be named Martha or Mary, nice dutiful female names! And how about my name, Germie dear? I'm so totally confused about my identity and sexuality I gave up worrying myself about it. I'm no jewel but I function all right. And anyhow—"

Now she scruffed the hair on the back of my skinny neck.

"—if little Patty here is giving herself the name of a problem, well, that's just honest. She is a problem. Sometimes you have to embrace death."

Germaine left after a couple more of Candy's remarks. She winked as she turned away. Funny thing was that she winked at *me*.

"Thanks for getting Dr. Means off me," I said to Candy. "But the whole business is upside down and you're the screwiest part of it. I don't know what you people want to do to me. I mean, I do know that you want me to accept this whole strange business.

"Take this weird tail I have." In the local area of the hospital I had given up running the damn thing down under my clothes. It was trailed out behind me. "I have been trying to cooperate by exercising it. Already I can curl it around something, though I can't adjust the grip. Can't really make it go where I want it. Strangest thing to have flesh where it can't be. I keep on trying to feel my way out to that emptiness at the end of my spine, or rather what used to be at the end of it. Maybe it's a little like those phantom pains people used to get in a missing leg before modern regeneration methods came in. Forget that.

"I have the same business with my new sex and the rest of this body. I'm surprised that Dr. Means hasn't already turned up at bedtime with some handsome male gorilla to exercise all my parts. So I accept. So I have sex in a female body. So I learn to be a gymnast with this new equipment. So I learn to dress and speak a little different and all that. It's all like some super feat. I know that you only get a few bodies a year to work with—Means said four in the Solar System last year—and they're mostly old bodies of suicides. After all, the premature death rate is one in a billion; I'm one in a billion if you count me that way. So the point is that I got a young body, which is a plus, but everything else is wrong. Sally Cadmus' body was just the best of bad choices.

"So why should I accept this? Why should I even try? I probably got a lot less than normal chances to make it through this. And if I make it through rejection, what have I got? I just don't like this. Feels itchy, all of me. Never stops. Like tiny snakes are crawling all over my skin. I want to succeed sometimes, I suppose, but what can I look forward to? I just can't get myself to care enough. There's a kind of distance, a fuzziness, about my sensations. Forget that, too."

Now I looked straight at Candy. While I was glaring I noticed that my tail, or rather the last foot or two of it, was swishing around in an arc just above the floor to the left and behind my chair.

"But—forget about me—what are you? Who are you? A lot of the time you are much too sarcastic and bright and—and everything—for someone your age, whatever it is. You look like a tall eleven-year-old girl. Fair skin and baby blond hair in antique braids, no less. Like a sky-maiden dream in one of Pardo's Vegan pop epics. But we all know you have got to be older than that by several years. And I'd be a total idiot if I didn't recognize that you got to be part of the therapy setup. Unless this is all some hallucination, you are fooling around with me in some sort of way. You and your fingers. What's your game, Candy?"

I continued to glare at Candy Darling at the end of this speech. But I was distracted by the swishing of the end of my tail, which had continued through my attack. My tail—the last foot or so of it, that is—flicked gracefully back and forth. This was some sort of automatic reflex. At least I had no control over it. And I couldn't yet produce such a controlled and sinuous movement.

"I have lots of games, Patricia," said Candy.

I didn't think that Candy had noticed the swishing. The table was between her and my tail. I managed to think the tail up. I got it hooked around my left knee.

"And I know what my games are and I'm going to talk to you about them. More than I can say for you, both ways. And then we'll get to you, Patty dear—"

I suddenly realized that I had never seen her face expressionless and motionless before. Her eyes seemed to lose their pigment.

"—for you know you won't find me as easy to deal with as Germaine. She's still young and soft-headed. Early forties. And you are?"

"I taped in at twenty-six, so that's my essential mental age, whatever happened to my body afterwards."

"And your body was thirty-one when it went into almost three years of low hibernation. The hibernation period doesn't really count, of course. At that temperature and chemical activity, mental function bleeds out. You get something like a 'blanked' brain in a few weeks, even without positive clearing. And the physical body respirates and ages at about an-hour-to-a-year rate. So let's say you're almost thirty. I am eighty years old, give or take a year or two, and I ain't no gullible softy. And I know your experience because I've been there. This is my sixth body."

It seemed almost as impossible as a stone cat grinning when one of her usual giggles flickered across her face.

"I'm a nympher, kid. One of the forty or so successful multiples in the Solar System, or the Federation for that matter. Nympher experience also helps me at my job. I'm a harmonizer and a reasonably good one, or so I'm told. In brief, I'm a sort of doctor and you're my patient. Such as you are. I'm also something else but we'll get to that later, big Patty. For now the subject is you."

Then Candy gave it to me.

"You think of yourself as rational and reasonable —sound mind and so on—except that you feel imprisoned in this body. You think of yourself as making a considered choice of name. And quite apart from that, you have made a reasonable survey of your situation and you don't like it. Death rather than dishonor. You are turning in your ticket and checking out with all . . . the dignity of a hysterical little brat."

Candy made a gesture with her hand as if introducing me to an audience with those last words. My hands went up in reflex or protest and then, moving under them, she got in a deft jab to my solar plexus. I doubled up just a bit. It was an accurate but light blow. And I saw that my tail had wound itself around her arm. Something in me was saying *Gotcha.*

"You are about as rational as a block of wood. You haven't asked the most basic questions about your situation. And you obviously haven't given any thought to your responsibilities."

"What responsibilities? My parents can more than take care of themselves and they are a hundred thousand light years from here, anyhow. I was just an off-and-on PR person for IBO. My friends can take care of themselves. I don't have any real responsibilities to anybody. If I die from rejection, that's it. I'm not a billionaire. So nobody gets hurt."

"How about this body, Patricia Forth?" Candy was pointing at me. "Have you got any idea of what rejection death will do to it? Do you care? Do you know how much I'm worth on the hoof?"

"Okay, okay," I said, "your body must be worth over a million credits—*if* you make it through your next implant to enjoy the money."

"It's worth what it's worth, whether I survive my next implant or not. That's the point you are forgetting. A body is worth so much because the only way we know how to produce one is the traditional way—and that takes years and years of exercise and experience, and it leaves you with an occupant. So aside from a one-in-a-billion character like me who's crazy enough to have her mind played into an infant every few months from birth until the brain is big enough to take the whole load, there's no source of bodies for implant except the rare suicide declaration. And who's interested in suicide when we can treat almost any psychological problem and can repair almost any physical disease, excepting total physical destruction? So the Sally Cadmus body is worth something like a million credits if you want to try to count. Rejection will make a mess of it."

"So who cares about a weirdo suicide body with this damn tail?" I said.

"You ought to, for one. That's one of the questions you haven't asked. You're occupying her body and you haven't shown one bit of curiosity about her. She's not a suicide, incidently. Possibly the only nonsuicide, nonnympher body ever implanted at NWRH. And the tail is a bioprosthesis—she must have got the thing started growing by adolescence. Must have been interesting how she got parental permission. She must have been a hellion. Anyhow, it's just exactly what someone needs when they work in weightlessness. She was an asteroid miner. It's not the money—that's just what we count by—you owe her, *you're responsible for her.* Though she's doing better by you so far."

"What do you mean?" I said. "Sally Cadmus is dead. I don't owe her anything."

"Forth, it is true that certain electrochemical patterns no longer exist in the cerebral cortex of the brain you happen to be rather inadequately occupying, but that's all. There's a lot of Sally Cadmus in the rest of the brain, and in the sense–motor system. Reflexes, unconscious skills, well-trained muscles, the whole bit. That's the Sally Cadmus you are responsible for. You got the body on trust."

"She gave it up, right?" I didn't feel too sure of myself, after Candy's statement that Sally Cadmus didn't suicide. Suicide declaration is about the only way I could see of a body coming free, apart from nymphing.

Candy Darling stood up and gestured me toward the door. "I'm going to show you what happened to Sally Cadmus. Might teach you a little respect for what you've been given, for what you are, in fact."

Candy got a small reel of tape from the VAT room with Austin Worms' help. We took it back to my room.

"Another thing you haven't asked about," said Candy as she inserted the tape into the room console. "Another thing you haven't asked one word about is what happened to the body you had—you don't know when it died, or where, or why, or even that it died. Sit down."

I sat. I should mention that the tape in question was just an ordinary recording tape, not one of those huge magnetic discs that can record the structure of a mind. Candy started a tape. There was static, as if one were hearing a long-range broadcast.

VII

A young, healthy blanked body is worth several million credits. You can buy a copy of your own mind tapes for less than a hundred credits—if you have any use for it, that is.

—I. F. + S. C. Operation Logbook, Append. III, The Chief's Report

"Hello, this is Sally Cadmus, prospector bond number delta-tau-seven-three-six-oh-two. Ship, *Baleen Blanco,* Federation registry number rho-nine-nine-seven-theta. This is a last statement.

"I was in-suit checking the surface of an outrider of Eros IV when my ship blew up. Probably just holed by a rock in the secondary fuel area. Bad luck in that I'm so far from the central belt that I'm a few hundred miles inside Earth's perihelion. Shouldn't get hit by space junk here. Funny to feel so far from help his close in the system.

"I figured Lamda Station was closest, but at near a hundred thousand miles their automatic-tracking screens wouldn't have even registered the blowup. I had my spares on my suit, about thirty-five hours of oxygen. Essentially no chance of survival.

"Ship compartment was totaled but I managed to scavenge the big external chem-fuel tank. The one I filled my suit tanks with. I cut the big tank free from the debris. Milked seven cuts out of my Alpha-Max, never did neater mincework in my life. I now have the big tank jury-tubed into my suit propulsion pack. In fact, up to now I've been hugging this twenty-five-foot tank as tight as possible. The propulsion unit pushes on the small of my back, almost a foot above the base of my tail, and with the unit on maximum thrust I've had to keep a hell of a good grip on all the inertia of the tank. It would weigh a couple of tons on Earth. Max thrust is over two hundred and fifty pounds, so I've had to be glued or I'd have been ripped away from this huge tank—which provided the fuel, so I had to take the bucking.

"My boots are still locked into some holder hooks and my gauntlets are clipped into a line of tube-fittings. The tube-fittings that ring the tank a fortunate two feet above its center of gravity. Since the rocket thrust from my unit goes through the small of my back and straight in front of me, I've had to balance the tank in front of me, letting the thrust push all of the front of me into the tank. Any other position and I would have pulled away. Locked on this way, I'd have to say it's lucky I had my tail to control the propulsion unit, particularly since the hose fitting from the big tank into the propulsion pack is a real patch job. I was bracing the fitting for most of the push. My tail still feels stiff, though I ran out of fuel fifteen minutes ago. I've got nothing to do but talk now.

"I figure I've had fuel to push this little unit for maybe twenty hours. Okay, nineteen twenty-two on my helmet timer. That's over fifty times more push than you normally carry on your pack. But all this is rough.

"Okay, whatever could mean the difference between cutting in on Earth from sunside or marside. In fact, more than Earth's diameter by a long shot. Plan is I'm going to curl wide round the sun so that I will catch a fat, slow curve outside Earth orbit. Let Earth catch up with me the second time around, giving her gravitational field good chances of picking me up. I've been astrogating by—I guess you might call it—the seat of my pants.

"I figured that there was no chance of me living but I can salvage something. Someone ought to get a body that isn't really beat up. If you are listening to this three years from now, I've got myself in the orbit I want. Fuel is gone. I don't know that I'd want to give this body the problem of living with a ten years' younger version of my mind. I specified that I didn't want implant when I got my majority. No tapes since.

"With fair luck this orbit should mean that I will catch Earth the second time she comes by this way. Earth has got so much sky junk they should pick up something as small as me and the tank. Biggest target I can aim at. If they can't pick me up coming in, you think Luna Station would? Luna has maybe seven to a dozen screens active—Earth must have like a couple thousand radar systems going. I can't aim myself well, so I need a big, sensitive target.

"Not too close to the sun, either. That's one advantage to the fat curve. I've arranged a foil heat baffle over me. But my main protection from heat is a kind of sea anchor, or rather solar wind anchor, trailing out a couple hundred feet behind me. A kind of sail that I hope will keep the tank between me and the sun by always pulling my side of the tank away from the sun.

"Okay, I'm messing around a lot, but I guess when there is something to save, you save. I specified nonrenewal on my majority tapes. They'd be ten years outdated. I am setting my suit pack to deep-hibernate me. The suit was checked through two months back and the Rossetti circuitry looks like it'll go a hundred years. I have retrieved the hibernation procedures and the declaration regulations on my suit computer. I guess I should make a formal statement.

"I, Sally Cadmus, let stand by my nonrenewal declaration. I understand that deep-hibernation procedure means the cessation of my mental structure. The higher electrochemical structure is randomly erased. I know that there is little chance of mental survival after even a few hours. You might as well give my estate to the implant.

"Good luck to her, anyhow. Hope she likes the tail. Useful. It's been a good time. She might . . .

"My beeper tells me I'm down to danger point on oxygen. My body needs some even for deep hibernation—breath a month. I'm hitting the circuit. Assume I've said the usual sentiments. Never could stand that stuff. Though I guess it may not be last *landing*. I'll be a shooting star if the screens don't pick me up far enough out.

"My solar wind anchor works. The tank is between me and the sun. The constellations are spread all around me. The great hunter Orion with his bright Dog. The Southern Cross. It's peculiar that us spacers are the first people since the invention of artificial lighting to be as familiar with them as the ancient Greek mariners and desert wanderers who named the constellations. My high school science teachers said the ancient Greeks foisted the constellations on us as arbitrary fantasies. Nothing connects the stars in Orion. They only give a vague outline of a hunter from Earth perspective, since some of Orion's stars are hundreds of light years away, while others are much, much farther. Just a matter of arbitrary perspective, or so he said.

"But Mr. Edgett never said it was arbitrary to call the sky blue. Yet the perspective for seeing the sky blue is a lot more narrow. You have to be somewhere in the narrow band of the Earth's lower atmosphere to see the sky as blue—a couple miles up and the sky starts to blacken. But you can see the hunter pattern we call Orion anywhere in the Solar System or near abouts. If there were Alpha Centaurians they could use the same constellations. I can use Ursa Major to get my bearings as well as the ancient Phoenicians. 'Magnetic north' has no more meaning to me than it did to them. The sky is black. And bright with figures. The ancients had no light to blind them to the stars. Gemini, Virgo, Taurus, the whole crew: light my way . . . Orion, hunter, mother . . ."

There was a long silence after Candy switched the tape off. I had never had the experience of space travel. I avoided flying, using flicks whenever possible. The one time I took a suborbital rocket to Singapore I got motion sickness. But I was struck by the sense of freedom that must go with weightlessness. The sense of being able to move with equal ease in any direction with no more effort than the mere flip of a tail. I thought of Sally Cadmus with nothing but endless space in all directions on her long orbit round the sun.

"How was her aim?" I asked Candy.

"As she figured," said Candy after she coughed and cleared her throat. "The station that picked you up reports that you were aimed so well that you would have gone into Earth orbit if they hadn't caught you. They also say that it is physiologically impossible for Sally to have had that good a sense of aim. According to those guys, human sights and reflexes could not have managed more than a thousand-to-one shot of coming anywhere near that close to Earth. You should still be up there by all rights, Patty Forth.

"And I've been sayin 'you' because, let's face it, you *are* the Sally Cadmus body, with nothing more than some electrochemical repatterning in the cerebral cortex. With nothing more than a tune from a tape labeled Ismael Forth."

VIII

Candy Darling remarked that the original Ismael Forth body, if undamaged, would fetch top credit on the zombie market.

—I. F. + S. C. Operation Logbook

I admit to being impressed by hearing Sally Cadmus' account of herself. Weightlessness had made me so sick on my Singapore rocket flight—a conference organized by my own Interplanetary Business Operations—that I switched to an ocean liner on my way back. I remember worrying about whether anyone would find out that I didn't take the rocket back. But the Sally Cadmus body—my body—had spent a lot of time in space.

I was standing at the in-town flicker just after the last important session of the Singapore conference broke up. I was hailed by none other than Norman Saylor Mather, the imperious and ancient ex-President and Board Chairman of IBO. I had been introduced to Chairman Mather some years ago by Uncle Wendel, a midmanagement type who got me into my IBO job. I was surprised that Mather had remembered me. But he hadn't remembered my name. He stood there with his hammy hands pinching my arms, saying, "Hah, you're young . . . young . . . look damn good, damn good, damn . . ."

"Ismael Forth," I eventually choked out.

I was worried that he might find out that I wasn't

taking the rocket back. Embarrassing. Last thing on my mind was the idea of taking advantage of this personal contact.

"That's fine—Ismael Forth, you say—that's fine, young fella, that's fine," he roared on. After a final "that's fine," he slammed me on the back once or twice, gabbed about college sports, and abruptly walked off. I slunk down to the flickerway, resolving never to allow myself to get into such a jaunt again. No rockets!

But now . . . Well, if I could take weightlessness now, I could stand up to the Norman Saylor Mathers of the universe. Do elegant acrobatics in free fall. Show the old coot. Come to think of it . . .

Candy brought me out of that reverie with a tug on the end of my tail.

"Like I said, kiddo, this goes the other way too," said Candy. She was perched on one end of my bed, her legs swinging back and forth, her hands still loosely holding my tail in her lap. Though she had returned to her usual precocious eleven-year-old voice, she had some disturbing things to say.

"It's strange that you didn't ask about where your new body came from. But it's a whole lot stranger that you didn't ask where your old body went. I told you—first time you woke up from the VAT operation—that you had been implanted and that you didn't have any estate or money problems. Do you realize, Patricia Forth, that since you've been awake you haven't asked what happened to your Ismael Forth body? Or when it happened, or where?"

I thought about it. Though I had daydreamed about the way my old, tall, well-muscled body looked—though I had definitely *yearned*—I had never actually asked myself what happened to the damn thing. Instead of hating my scrawny new body and demanding that my poor tail be cut off, why hadn't I screamed for my old body? Or at least asked what had happened to it? After all, the sort of total body wipeout that called for the risks and problems of implantation was a one-in-a-billion event. I should have been curious. I was curious now.

"So what did happen?" I said. "You know, Candy, that all I got are memories up to that yearly tape update. I don't have a clue in that about any dangers. And doing a little PR work for IBO—Interplanetary Business Operations—wouldn't mean any risks. And I didn't have any dangerous hobbies like mountain climbing, lung diving, or sky sports. To tell the truth I was more careful of myself than most people, though I kept myself in good shape . . . I mean I kept the Ismael Forth body in good shape."

Let's see now, I thought to myself, they must have been planning the operation for months. I had Ismael Forth memories until my tape update in January, 2111. Sometime later in 2111 something happened to my earlier body. Something conclusive. Candy was looking at one of the pink sheets from my medical file.

"There is not as much information here as there might be because you died on Rim. No regular autopsy and scavenger program, as you would get in a civilized place, so we don't know anything much. All this says is that you traveled as a tourist to Rim, landing there at Xanadu on July eighth, 2111 A.D., and that you died by drowning near there on July fourteenth. Now, what do you think of that?"

Candy Darling patted my tail as if she expected it to answer.

I was dumbfounded. I couldn't even recall having heard of a place called Rim. It certainly isn't in North America, I thought.

"What on Earth is Rim?" I asked.

"It's not on Earth at all, dummy. Rim is the nearest Earthlike planet to the new Canopus wormhole. Federation's put a stop on any development except for a small resort area—*very* exclusive—around Xanadu."

"I have never heard of the place. And besides I never—"

Candy Darling cut off the beginning of my confession. "Hold it, Patty Forth, give yourself time to think. I got at least two reasons to think you should've heard of Rim. First is that your company, IBO, actually controls most of Xanadu and the surrounding area, and is interested in the potential mass development of Rim. Of course neither IBO nor the Federation conservationists have an interest in publicizing Rim much now. But you should have heard of the place, working for IBO—"

"But, Candy," I broke in, "I've *never been in space.* I *never* would—I mean Ismael Forth never would—have taken a spaceflight. The only time I experienced weightlessness I was so sick I swore I would never do it again. When I was Ismael Forth wild monsters wouldn't have driven me into space. Anyhow, how could I have afforded an interstellar trip?"

Candy looked at me quizzically.

"Would it help," she said, "if I told you that my second reason for thinking that you might have heard of Rim is that you won an IBO employee lottery for an all-expenses-paid vacation on 'the exclusive, someday-to-be-developed wonderworld' of Rim? Here, look at this."

Candy had a clipping in her hand. She did not hand it up the bed toward my extended hands. She held the clipping over the end of my tail.

I am sure you don't know how it feels to grab something with your own prehensile tail. ("Prehensile tail" means one that can encircle and grasp an object. The South American monkeys have such tails, though African, Asiatic, and Vegan monkeys do not.) To me my tail feels as if the last foot or so were longer and bigger than all the rest of it. The last foot really *feels.* I had been trying to learn how to grasp things with my tail for days without success.

I guess it was just a case of thinking too hard. Of worrying about success. In any case, I grabbed the clipping from Candy's hand with my tail and had it in front of my face before I realized what was happening. Automatic reflexes.

I was too interested in the clipping to think about my new achievement. The clipping was from the IBO in-house newsletter, *The Iboer*, dated June thirtieth of last year.

IBO PR MAN OVERWHELMED BY SURPRISE VACATION PRIZE

Ismael Forth won't be working or seeing friends the next few days. He'll be too busy preparing for the trip of a lifetime, an all-expenses-paid two-week vacation on fabulous Rim, a virgin wilderness world billions of miles from Earth. Lucky Ismael Forth will be hobnobbing with the small number of rich and powerful sophisticates who have visited Xanadu, the one spot of luxury and civilization that the Federation allows on Rim. Someday IBO will make this wonderworld available to all of us.

"I never expected to win a prize like this," said Ismael at his home yesterday. "Tell them I'll bring back a bug-eyed monster to put on the lunchroom wall." Have fun, Ismael!

Though I recognized the typeface and style of the old *Iboer,* I somehow didn't take in the point of the article at once. The first thing that occurred to me was that the line that IBO was someday making "this wonderworld available to all of us" was a load of syrup. The fact of the matter is that while a lot of people have taken a trip or two inside the Solar System, not many people can afford interstellar flight. Interstellar flight belongs to the immigrants, the good old rich and powerful, and the professionals—the explorers, scientists, and military types of the Federation, and of course the wormhole flight crews themselves.

My parents, for example, took bonded passage as immigrants to Osiris, out the Procyon wormhole. We would not have been likely to see one another again even if I had remained Ismael Forth and had conquered my space sickness. Interstellar flight was just too costly. Realistically, there is only a difference in tone between "interstellar" and "wormhole." "Interstellar" means between-stars, while "wormhole flight" means via-whatever-it-is-that-connects-some-of-this-universe's-space-time-with-others-in-absolute-simultaneity-outside-Einsteinian-reality. But the one way to make an interstellar flight that does not require several lifetimes is by wormhole flight, so in practice the two are the same.

And then, as you would be expecting, I finally took in the whole clipping—and felt little shivers all the way down my spine. Tail, too. An undulation which terminated in a reflexive whipping motion of the tip.

Space flight and weightlessness. And wormhole flight as well.

"But, Candy," I said, "that's impossible. I told you, my old body—Ismael Forth—was never in space. I got very sick on my only suborbital flight. Very embarrassing not to be able to take weightlessness at all. I would never have gone to Rim even if the trip were free. This article from the *Iboer . . .*"

I had intended to say that the article was crazy. But I stopped as I realized that Candy was rhythmically squeezing the end of my tail. The rhythm was the universal three shorts—in this case pinches—followed by three longs and another three shorts. SOS.

When I stared at Candy her finger briefly touched her lips. After the pinching I recognized that the finger must mean silence. If someone had had a video hologram of Candy Darling and me, they would not have noticed Candy's gesture.

Candy took what looked like a palmsize computer-video from her bag. She punched several addresses on the keyboard, listening to random static after each operation. Then she took the back off the computer-video and punched some internal buttons.

You can't take the back off a normal computer-video. And you certainly can't take the back off a cheap, rainbow-colored, Maizie-the-Cow children's model.

Candy now leaned back, relaxed, on the bottom of my bed.

"Not," she said, "that I really thought that anyone was bugging us. But rules have to be followed and they say I got to clear an area before I talk openly to anyone. Patty, girl, I am not only a harmonizer, I am an investigator for the Federation."

Candy Darling gave me a glowing and invincible eleven-year-old grin. Like the cat with chicken feathers in its teeth.

"You see, Patty, a prepubertic girl with a very adult and cynical mind makes a very good spy indeed. Sort of Shirley Holmes peeping out of Alice in Wonderland's eyes."

At this point Candy gave me a peculiar look that was probably intended to suggest just such a combination—the astute mind leering cynically out of its innocent casing. I understood how effective the disguise was: a blond-haired, blue-eyed, eleven-year-old girl simply cannot look like a jaded and ingenious detective. Even if she is.

"What it comes to is this," continued Candy. "Your Ismael Forth body is one of several that have disappeared in an odd way in the past two years. The *odd way* is that they have all suffered so-called accidents that either wiped out all trace of the body—explosions and the like—or the body dies in a frontier place like

Rim, where routine medical procedures—autopsy, gene identification, scavenging, and other ghoulwork —won't be done. There are other suspicious circumstances. But your, Ismael's, inability to take weightlessness is a mighty glaring clue. You would never have walked your Ismael Forth body on board a spaceship. So *you* didn't go on board. But the body did. And wasn't seen too often after departure on the F.S. *Pequod* by my information . . ."

Body-snatching. Zombies.

Candy didn't actually say the word *body-snatching.* It just hung in the air. So that was what it was really all about. The bastards had taken my old body.

Suddenly I felt my horror turn into a cold, clear hatred. For the first time since I had been awakened by Candy Darling I felt fully alive and hot with purpose. I was awake.

"How?" I said.

"Well, Patty dear," replied that girlish and eerie voice, "it's something that we always knew could be done. You know that the Federation doesn't allow implants after a mind has reached an essential age of eighty-five. That's the Kellog-Murphy Bill again. One reason we don't allow those late implants is that they don't work well. You get less than the normal four-in-five chance of surviving body-mind rejection. And some of the successful ones begin to go bad in a few months. But the other big reason is that people's bodies—originals—begin to start to break down after eighty-five or ninety or so, even with all the preservation techniques we got. So some people might want to take a risk in their nineties, a last fling.

"As Counselor Kellog said, 'It is impossible to distribute that mixed blessing fairly, given the few donor bodies available and the expense of the operation; so it must not be distributed at all.'

"What a very few people know is that you can press a few years beyond essential mind death—if you can pay the cost. The cost is frequent implants and a kind of paranoia. You need a whole lot of money and something like a private army and a VAT implant operation of your very own."

I can testify that the sweat of a young body with an ancient mind smells sweet. Lack of development of the sweat glands that come with puberty, I suppose.

Candy wriggled up the bed. An observer would have seen a classical mother-daughter or older-younger sister scene. Candy had her head nestled on my breast. I could feel an interesting and irritating tingle in the nipple. And I was quite conscious that Candy's knee was slipping, as she talked to me, from my bellybutton down between my legs.

"We think," she whispered, "that we might find out something by checking out Rim. And you do happen to know what the Ismael Forth body looks like.

"Germaine has said you spent some time looking at your old self in sauna mirrors. The only photographs we've been able to get of you are several years out of date. And I would need a decoy companion in my case. People my age don't go on interstellar voyages alone. No one will recognize your new body or wonder who you might be, if you act like a normal zenith-class tourist.

"Are you game, Patty?"

I didn't know whether I wanted to have sex or an expedition with Candy Darling. But I was her woman.

"Let's get 'em" is what I said.

And we did.

IX

"Motivation is crucial," remarked François Vase. "We have got to give her every reason to want to live."

—I. F. + S. C. Operation Logbook

The most satisfying experience of the next two days was to walk past Dr. Means, down the elevator, and out of the door of the Norbert Wiener Research Hospital. Not that Dr. Means was as sticky about it as you would expect. As a rather more traditional male than usual on Earth I had rather disliked a modern woman like Dr. Means. But she wears well. Worms, the head ghoul, was full of advice about exercise and infections and all that sort of stuff. Weird to think that he had handled me, exercised and patted me, for months before the implant. But Dr. Means didn't protest after Candy and I made it clear we were going, and she shook our hands rather gravely as we left.

The most interesting experience was acquiring a wardrobe—unless you count our discovery of what Candy called "the telltale tail."

Candy's plan of action came to this: we would not mess around with IBO here. I was a closed issue to them. Ismael Forth was dead. No point in reopening that. We made a good pair of investigators. Or, rather, I was a good cover for Candy.

We would travel to Rim on the F.S. *Pequod*. Same ship that the Ismael Forth body traveled on. Same crew. Might be able to dig up some information on how the body had behaved. Zombies—bodies without minds—could be rigged up to look conscious and walk about, but there were all sorts of telltales. And there would have been someone on board who had minded the Ismael Forth body. We would want to know who that was, or who they were, if there were more than one. After we got to Rim we would try to figure out what had really happened to the Ismael Forth body. Within the restricted area allowed it by the Federation, Xanadu was supposed to have the beginnings of the most exclusive of the interstellar-set resorts. I was looking forward to that.

But there were problems in the plan. Candy pointed them out before we left NWRH. The one we argued about was what identities we should assume. Candy Darling would have little difficulty passing as a ten-year-old. All she had to do was watch her mouth. Watch about slipping into talking like a cynical adult, but she was used to that. What Candy said was that most kids really have adult minds by the age of ten or so, and most adults, parents particularly, try to ignore this state of affairs. So Candy figured that she had no problem passing off an adult mind in a kid's body because that's what "normal" ten-year-olds are doing anyhow. Sounds reasonable if you think about it.

But Candy needed to travel with someone. And I was needed to make an identification in any case, so I would be the traveling companion. The question was, What sort of traveling companion?

I had my hands full being a female. Who was I to complain at being a mother in addition?

Candy made a convincing case on the basis of ages, though I think she enjoyed the idea too, the little son of a ——— (daughter of a ———?). I had no idea of the sex of the body Candy had started out with.

My body was, physically, thirty-one. And it looked that old too. At least that's what Candy said. At the time I had no opinion about how it looked. I avoided mirrors like someone might avoid the eye of a basilisk.

So I was thirty-one and Candy was, or looked to be, eleven. What could be more innocent, or more likely, than that we should be mother and daughter? Who was I to protest?

One thing you have to get straight if you're to follow this account is that Candy was leading me around by the hand through this whole period. I suppose a few children dominate their parents in such a manner. I don't know how else to explain the way Candy took me shopping.

"Let's make Mommy" was what she chirped in my ear as she pushed into Houston's Rostard's, a stylish millionaire's clothier far beyond my previous experience.

"Dress her well, M. Herbert," is what she said to the elegant gentleman who rushed up to greet her after we entered the store. And dress me (or it) is what Herbert proceeded to do—as if he were handling a clothing dummy, or perhaps merely someone heavily sedated. He must have dealt with odd clients of Candy's before. He made some comment about looking forward to dressing her up when she reached adolescence *again*. He must have known her before she had her present body.

The wardrobe was constructed in a private suite. Herbert scurried in and out while Candy slipped from her authoritatively adult manner (to Herbert) to her sassy little darling style (to me). I—the Patricia Forth body, that is—just stood there, moving the limbs about when they asked me to. I had hoped that my tail, at least, would disturb the suave M. Herbert. But it dismayed him no more than my nudity or being ordered about by an eleven-year-old girl.

First of all a decision had to be made about what

to do with the tail. The loose pants I had been wearing around the hospital allowed me to conceal it by stuffing it down one leg into a loose-fitting boot top. But you can't be wearing pants and boots all the time. You certainly can't wear them all the time on a luxury liner. Especially when you are rolling in credits.

You had to give it to M. Herbert, though. When they got my clothes off and he saw the tail, his first reaction was artistic. He saw it as a unique providence, almost a challenge. He wanted to leave it in plain view. In fact he wanted to create a new style in clothing around it.

"After I have finished and they have seen the ensemble, the stylish ladies will want fake tails just to be able to wear the new style. She will be regal, an exotic princess, a queen, an empress from afar . . ." He went on for some time like that, fondling my tail and positively glowing as he speculated about what jewelry would fit the tip of it.

He went so far as to argue with Candy about it until she shut him up. Candy took the view that we were to be inconspicuous and untraceable. So the tail must be hidden. And we were to be wealthy. Who but the wealthy would be riding the *Pequod* to Rim? And who but such a passenger could be expected to put forward a zenith display of fashion? I must have all sorts of clothing, much of it for display and social occasions. So dresses, shirts, skirts, and tolongs were the order of the day. And while I was to be a mother, I was also to be a beautifully and commandingly dressed young woman.

Candy put it another way. "You're a regular red-hot momma, Momma," she said while I was modeling a particularly dashing black evening gown. The gown's cloaklike lines more resembled a tolong than a dress. Except that the (my) breasts were bare.

Because of the tail, Herbert had to select from among tolongs, reasonably loose pants, and skirts and dresses that flared at the waist or buttocks. When my legs were to be bare they wrapped the tail between the legs and around the belly. The whole business of the tail still made me sick. I still wanted it off, whatever Dr. Means said about that making my brain go sick. I was even less some sort of monkey than a woman. But I could move the tail. (Think of moving the little bone at the end of your spine. And think that feeling out the back of you. A long curling and winding cylinder. And finally put something that feels like your index finger and a bit of thumb at the end.)

It just didn't feel right to have this whole appendage, my appendage, wrapped around me like a jockstrap or a belt. It didn't want to be that way.

I didn't feel quite the same way about the brassieres. Though the dead lumps on my chest didn't feel as large or as horrible or even as cancerous as at first. It felt better having a brassiere over them. Like having them packed away in two form-fitting elastic bandages.

But otherwise I didn't feel happy with the frilly underwear that M. Herbert and Candy went in for. And it wasn't simply *me*, you know. It was also the skin I was walking around inside of. I felt weird about the silky nonabsorbent stuff just because it was for a woman, and mostly for dress and party occasions. I had run into it before only in sexual fumblings—and then, of course, from the other side of the fence, so to speak. But it seemed somehow that my skin didn't like it either. Itchy in some funny way. I don't think Sally Cadmus would have worn that sort of stuff.

I couldn't say more than "itchy in some funny way" because I was still going through all sorts of tuning with my senses. I was slowly working together what I felt inside when one sense or another got pushed by what was out there. When I first had mustard on my tongue, for example, my mind gave me the smell and feel of turpentine. After several weeks that changed too. It wasn't so much that the actual taste changed. As if it tasted just a bit like turpentine, but it *was mustard*. Yellow, tangy, belongs on dubers. That came to be the way mustard was supposed to taste.

Your senses are tuned. All hooked up to the world by years of smelling, seeing, tasting, touching, moving, and working with objects out there. But I was still all out of whack that way.

Plus I had a new tail and even what you might call a new sense. That's the business of what Candy called the "telltale tail." It happened right there while they were trying the clothes on me. It's important for what happens later.

M. Herbert had just removed a white linen tolong from my body. The tolong was too loose and flowing to be very practical. Apparently it was suitable wear for garden parties but not after dark. Sol knows why Candy and Herbert thought I needed such an item. They couldn't have garden parties on the F.S. *Pequod*. (I was wrong about that last point, as you'll see.)

Candy and Herbert were speculating as to whether I should get another tolong of the same style but some other color. And I was free to stretch my legs and tail. Without clothes I would walk with the tail curving down behind me to within a few centimeters of the floor, with the sensitive tip curving up (and often weaving from side to side in an inquisitive manner).

As I passed by the back wall of the suite, the tip of my tail felt something that is hard to describe.

Imagine an intelligent extraterrestrial creature who could *see* ultraviolet rays. Then imagine that creature trying to explain to us what color ultraviolet was. But what happened to me was harder to relate because at least we know some of the color spectrum—ultraviolet is just up the spectrum a little beyond what we humans can see.

But imagine a wholly different sense. Like bats, who *see* the things around them in all directions by bouncing high-pitched sounds off them. Or like the many fish who can sense other fishes' magnetic fields.

What it felt like was something like this: I felt as if my tail was bathed in some sort of yellowish light. At the same time I got a feeling as if the whole assemblage, from tail tip up to the bottom of my spine, were a mouth that was puckered up by testing something really astringent, like alum. And I also had the strange feeling that I was smelling something putrid. I leaped away.

At the moment that this combination of feelings hit me, the tip of my tail was a few centimeters from what looked to be an inconspicuous light switch on the back wall. Curious, I moved back, slowly flexing my tail toward the switch area. I swished my tail back and forth. The same weird combination of sensations occurred whenever the tip of my tail came within a few centimeters of the light switch.

I wasn't sensitive to light switches, I was sure. I'd already met up with plenty of them. There was something different about this light switch.

"Caught something, Patricia?" said Candy, coming up behind me.

"There's something funny about this light switch. My tail reacts to it."

"Ah, yes, my lady," said M. Herbert somewhat apologetically as he waddled up, wringing his hands. It was the first remark that he had addressed to me since I had entered the store.

"You see, my lady, it is sometimes necessary for one such as myself to be more cautious than you might assume. All is not as simple as it looks."

He held his hands up and pursed his lips in a gesture at the complications of galactic mercantilism.

"Certainly Mme. Candy here is hardly what she would seem.

"And you, my charming lady with the tail. You, I suspect, are not as you seem."

He favored me with a smile that suggested we were part of some elegant conspiracy. Then he did something complicated with the light switch and the plate that held it on the wall. The plate popped out of the wall. M. Herbert turned to us, his hands outward, palms up, the way a magician holds them after a trick. I could not resist applauding.

Candy examined the efficient gun-metal-and-glass device that looked out from where the plate had been.

"A Zeiss-Telemark spy scope," said Candy. "And with the full microstat capacity too. You have expensive tastes, M. Herbert.'"

"At Rostard's we have the best always," replied Herbert. He bowed.

I swept out of Rostard's encased in an impeccably austere, steel-gray tolong whose simple lines carried all the authority of four centuries of French tailoring.

"Your tail looks to be sensitive to the spy-scope range of electromagnetic radiation," said Candy. "Maybe the damn thing will have a useful function after all."

"You could say, Mommy-poo . . ."

Here she smiled up at me cherubically while sneaking a swift pinch to my buttocks.

"You could say that you have a telltale tail."

My punch missed.

X

A prehensile tail is found only among small monkeys. A large monkey cannot have a tail strong enough to be an independent support for tree travel, just as a bird as big as an ostrich cannot afford wings strong enough for flying. In weightlessness, however . . .

—I. F. + S. C. Operation Logbook

I must say that if my former body had any sort of consciousness when it (he?) traveled to Rim, it must have enjoyed the marshaling of the stewards.

Ensconced in an elegant, virginal white tolong, Candy bore herself with all the grace and dutifulness that one might expect of a real eleven-year-old aristocratic daughter. She sat, legs straight and together, to my left in the thin dawn-shimmering air of Rocky Mountain Raiser Port. To my right, feet separated by the regulation thirty centimeters, hands clasped behind, stood the F.S. *Pequod*'s First Officer, Duncan Hanney Starbuck. The dazzlingly white collar that protruded from his deep-blue dress uniform might have been as stiff as his spine. But I doubted it.

I stood, my left hand in maternal grace on Candy's shoulder. I wore a tweed cloak of pale-gray Vegan sky sheep. You would not only have thought that Mrs. Patricia Forth had money and lots of it; unconsciously you would have felt that the money had been transmuted into grace and casual authority through generations. M. Herbert had done his job. It was not an accident that First Officer Duncan Starbuck had chosen to attend me on the resplendently polished oakwood quarterdeck of the Rocky Mountain Raiser. He had hardly paused to chat with two or three passengers before introducing himself. Nor was it an accident that he should have personally insisted on fetching a chair for Candy. He came close to apologizing for the fact that Captain Mathew A. Brainbridge was already aboard the *Pequod,* orbiting the earth in company with Space Station Zebra, some hundreds of kilometers above us.

For several minutes now, khaki-clad teams of raiser crew members had been bustling about. Their movements were punctuated by the shrill squeals of bosuns' whistles. Already the raiser was lighter than air, the vast platform swaying slightly and ponderously in the early morning air. The platform was shackled to earth by a hundred lines. The crew's activity ensured that it was pulled upward directly by the score of balloons fettered to its peripheries. The raiser was the size of a midcity block. It was flat, with two exceptions.

One was the quarterdeck where we stood. The other, at the platform's center, was the gigantic packet catapult. The catapult would hurtle into space the passengers, the stewards, and the still-Earthside portion of the *Pequod*'s crew. The compressed air catapult ensured that the packet ship's rocket did not blow to bits the vast but delicate structure of the raiser platform. Or explode the superlight hydrogen that filled its balloons.

Diffidently, First Officer Starbuck explained that early spaceships blasted their way into space with an unspeakably enormous expenditure of fossil-product energy. And with a criminally mad production of atmospheric pollution. In those days overland jet flights were permitted. And ocean transports employed fossil-fuel engines rather than the sails of modern vessels.

"I don't mean just in harbor or on a lee shore,

where we employ electric engines," said First Officer Starbuck, his voice dropping to a whisper. "They didn't even use sails in normal sailing conditions." His voice now sunk to near inaudibility. "They didn't even *have* sails."

He was looking away from me. If anything, his spine was stiffer than before. The tightening of the muscles in his face gave his profile a sculptured look, emphasizing his cheekbones.

The regal figure of Chief Steward Ernest Inger appeared below us at the peak of the raiser's waist. He was resplendent in his starched white uniform decked with gold braid. With a clear but respectful sense of relish in the importance of his gesture, he put his silver whistle to his lips as a conductor might raise his baton. Two measured blasts and the bustle of the crew of the raiser subsided into silence. He put the whistle to his lips for a third blast and a mad twittering of hornpipes coincided with his whistle. Simultaneously, the twenty stewards of the F.S. *Pequod* appeared in uniforms only marginally less splendid than that of their chief. They popped as one from under the conning shed and quick-marched in unison to the pipes to the raiser's ladders. Even the climb had a balletic precision. As the pipes ascended to a final pitch of ecstatic madness, the paired groups of ten stewards strode up two gangways from the lower deck to the waist, crossing each other in the ascent in a brilliant harmony of white and gold. The piping ceased precisely as they marshaled into rigid attention before the Chief Steward.

"That is about all they are capable of doing," said First Officer Duncan Starbuck. "Aside from being able to bring you a poached egg before it cools. Keeps them in condition."

"But it is charming," I said in my best new manner. As if charming was something that menials and small children did when suitably motivated. Not something that an officer or woman of breeding would dream of undertaking.

I was rewarded with a warm smile from Officer Starbuck. Candy winked at me. She was probably feeling restless as Mistress Candice Armitage Forth, daughter of Mrs. Patricia Cabot Armitage Forth. Imposing, regal, excellent. I would have intimidated *you.*

"Warp and toggle her, Mr. Nichols," said First Officer Starbuck as the packet settled into the gigantic bulk of the *Pequod.* His voice took on a less commanding tone. "Gentlepersons, the brief period of weightlessness will soon be over."

To tell the truth even the gentle and ponderous swaying of the raiser platform had begun to make me worry about space sickness. I had never experienced weightlessness. Even jet travel made *me* queasy. Maybe I should put that another way: the Ismael Forth body had never spaced.

I really began to worry when we were nested down in the closely packed seats of the tiny packet boat. As the thousands of elastic filaments settled over me, I hardly heard the encouraging comments of Chief Steward Inger. The packet was as jammed with people as a pomegranate with seeds; the twenty-one stewards, other members of *Pequod*'s crew, and the twoscore or so passengers. The passenger and conning compartment of the packet took up over a third of her length. The engines and fuel that took up the rest of her thirty-meter length were just sufficient to lift her slantwise a few kilometers into the stratosphere. Unassisted, she would then inevitably have begun to sink and soon plummet to earth. But assistance was to be had.

Space Station Zebra, dropping into the radical nadir of its orbit, would catch the packet. Imagine an osprey diving on a fish that leaped above the ocean's surface, only to sweep upward into the blue once again.

"Catch" is the operative word, for the huge station and the tiny packet are no match in speed or direction. The packet has spent its force and is at the point of sinking downward, while the station, having reached the lowest point of its orbit, is just to begin its sweep away from the Earth.

Zebra, like most space stations, was shaped like a doughnut. Unlike the deep-space ship *Pequod,* which it would rejoin after reaching halfway to its apogee, Zebra was streamlined for its sweep through the middle atmosphere. The packet was caught in an elaborately structured web in the hole of the doughnut. As if the navigational problem were not enough, there was a further complication. The station was cartwheeling around its axis to maintain a modicum of gravity for the occupants of the doughnut.

"This packet is a *boat,"* I heard the First Officer correcting a passenger. "Not a ship, like *Pequod.* A boat is conned by a pilot, while a ship's direction is the responsibility of the Captain, the bridge officers, and the navigator. Both a boat and a ship are *shes.*

"The station is an *it,"* he added didactically. I was beginning to enjoy Starbuck.

Several of the passengers gasped as the compressed air of the catapult slammed us skyward. A boyish voice screamed. The momentary pressure on my back and tail felt strangely reassuring. I felt balanced somehow as the lesser pressure of the packet's rocket phased in. Like the ascent a dancer feels when her partner helps her rise with his palm thrusting up the small of her back. I felt the sort of tingle that runs through you just before you sneeze.

You hardly have a chance to grow used to the motion of the packet before it slams into the web of the station. And then the stewards are bustling about rapidly, jostling the passengers up and into the joist tube, which snakes out through the webbing of the station.

The idea is to get the passengers into the artificial gravity of the station fast, before they feel the effects of their rapidly declining weight.

The boy who had screamed looked quite green. His eyes wobbled. Chief Steward Inger and I helped him into the tube. I beamed at Candy. She looked like she was sucking a lemon.

"Thank you very much indeed, my lady," said Chief Inger, tipping his hat. We completed our entry into the near-Earth-level gravity of the doughnut portion of Space Station Zebra. Inger smiled deferentially.

"I believe, my lady, that it was the poor tyke's first time in space. One doesn't quite know how they will react. I'm sure you've seen such cases. And I'm sure he'll come round promptly. If not, Doc will put him right."

Chief Inger tapped the braid on his cap once more. "I'll keep an eye on him for you, my lady."

Real weightlessness came two hours later. Zebra had matched orbits with *Pequod*. We reentered the tiny packet, now moored on the outside of the doughnut. We were propelled gently into the gigantic bulk of the *Pequod*, which looked like a dumbbell festooned with countless masts, antennae, and reception cones. There was unavoidable weightlessness for the very brief period from the warp in of the packet until we were once again bustled off into the weighted passenger areas of the *Pequod*. Weightlessness.

Five full minutes of weightlessness before finally, apologetically, First Officer Duncan Starbuck insisted that I must leave the weightless packet boat because he couldn't exit the packet until the last of the passengers had left.

I felt the tingles washing through me much more strongly this time. The tip of my tail felt hot. Weightlessness. It washed over me. Like Mom, Dad, the old

Howard frizzie theater, Julie's pale-green eyes, the warm drowsy feel of the old backyard Klein-closure—like all there is that renews us and protects us and is us, my thoughts cascading to my body's rhythms. Weightlessness.

Home.

XI

It is impossible to tune mind and body in isolation. They must play upon each other and the world.

—I. F. + S. C. Operation Logbook, Append. II, Press Releases

Chief Engineer Trudy Double sauntered up to the Captain's table in *Pequod*'s dining salon. Her unaccustomed interruption momentarily scattered the solemn rituals of the three stewards who hovered about our table. She bent down past my left side to whisper something to Captain Mathew A. Brainbridge.

"Yes, yes, Chief," he said discreetly. "Of course. And have Ernest tell the galley to lay on something special."

He cleared his throat deliberately and smiled expansively to the table, once more the genial host. His fair and florid skin curved a touch too loosely over his tall frame.

As Officer Starbuck might have put it, the apposition of "Chief" and "Ernest" made a distinction age-old to ships. Engineer Double belonged to the real crew of the *Pequod*, the men and women who conned her computers, juggled the nonstandard numbers representing her impending wormhole trajectory, worried over her running gear, and maintained the atomic fires of the power end of her dumbbell structure, holding fusion reactions of temperatures over two million degrees Celsius in spidery webs of magnetism. Chief Engineer Trudy Double was, at the most informal, simply *Chief,* as Duncan Starbuck was *First* and Captain Brainbridge *Captain.* Even the lowliest member of Chief Double's six-person staff, Mate Victor Blout, was always at least *Mate,* or *Blout,* never *Victor.*

Ernest Inger was chief of the entire staff concerned with pleasuring the passengers, maintaining the living quarters, and feeding the crew. And he was a cornucopia of regal dignity and ponderous gentility. Yet the Chief Steward was *Ernest.* He was deferred to by all but the senior officers. Chief Double was a six-footer with the agility of a space-born gymnast, and she did not suffer fools gladly or for long. Yet Ernest Inger could speak to Chief Double in the manner of a sententious uncle. But to Chief Double as much as to the Captain—indeed, to the lowliest of the officers—he was *Ernest.* Always and ever *Ernest.*

The Captain paused while the stewards served the dacca. This dacca was a golden, tongue-tingling variety. The Chief Steward confided that it was brewed only in far Permio, outside the official reach of the Federation. The dacca was poured from an antique pewter pitcher into goblets of light-rose-colored diamond, spun to paper thinness and tensile strength by the diamond blowers of New Holland. The golden dacca frothed against the pale rose of the diamond goblets.

The steward pouring the dacca paused over Candy's glass.

"I should like you to try some, Candice," I said to her, thus removing the steward's indecision. "And you will want to have some of that black cheese on the thin wafers, too."

Our stateroom contained three books about haute cuisine and zenith-class life style. Even Candy had never eaten the classic accompaniment for expensive dacca. The black cheeselike stuff—*glenna un petit*—was extracted from the anal glands of a Vegan weasel-like creature. It cost three thousand credits a kilogram Earthside. I spooned a generous portion onto my plate.

"You will find that it tastes like fine chanterelle mushrooms, my dear. Something of the consistency of a creamy cheese like Brie, though, Candice." I spoke with stealthy confidence. Horvath's *Galactic Gastronomique* is an amusing and engrossing book when read in the right spirit.

"Thank you, Mother."

"I should try just a smidgen, Candy," said Captain Brainbridge. He leaned across me to smile at her. His knee brushed mine.

The Captain cleared his throat again. His eyes circled the table, the Captain's table, from left to right. The Corns and the Piggs, five Texans whose New Houstonian money gilded their lack of sophistication or restraint into myth-proportioned eccentricity. Isa Pigg V had once Earth-heaved a Matterhorn-sized mountain into the San Hernandez Fault to change the view from her ancestral mansion north of Austin, Texas. Then three youngish Mathers, heirs to the IBO money. Third Officer Stubb, a handsome and presentable young man, who was imported from the Navigator's table in order to balance our table sexually. And Candice Armitage Forth. And me, to Captain Mathew A. Brainbridge's right.

"The *Pequod* will enter the Canopus wormhole sometime tomorrow afternoon. It is a tradition of space to have some festivity during wormhole flight." Captain Brainbridge's voice became more confiding.

"As those of you who have experienced it know, wormhole flight is a kind of initiation. And a most pleasurable one, I assure you." He smiled at me. Under my tolong my tail itched.

"The non-Einsteinian weave of wormhole space has a curious effect on the human nervous system. You are likely to feel just a touch giddy, a touch warm.

"We had planned a somewhat more sumptuous dinner than usual." He gestured as if apologizing that the meal we had just enjoyed consisted of something like oily algae burgers.

"And a party of sorts. But Trudy Double, our Chief Engineer, has suggested that we make the party a masked costume ball.

"Now, you may feel that this is a silly business." He smiled. "And of course it is. But I assure you that wormhole flight is conducive to such silliness. You won't feel silly while it is happening, just effervescent.

"And perhaps"—he winked—"perhaps a trifle amorous."

My knee felt his again.

The *glenna un petit* tasted like rotten cocktail onions. Horvath's *Galactic Gastronomique* is not infallible.

"He's attracted to you, all right," said Candy from the antique ottoman on which she sprawled. She sucked absent-mindedly on the oily-smelling Vegan cannabis that she favored.

"He loves to talk about you. Boring. Mistress Forth this and Mistress Forth that. And you're not all that sexy. Just magisterial and exotic. But *you'll* never get anything out of First Officer Duncan Starbuck. He would probably be unable to speak if you held his hand. And if you touched his cock, he'd probably burst half his blood vessels.

"Me he can talk to. And talk he do. Trajectories, storage of dress uniforms, wardrobe suppers, null-transfer bisections, off-point Hendersen flanges, hyperspace Holmann orbits, wormhole isolation, proper officer's kit packing.

"I just try to steer him a little bit—big blue eyes looking up worshipfully." The bluish smoke eddied upward.

Candy continued in her best little-girl voice:

"Gee, what's that, Dunkie?

"That's awful weird-looking. What does it do?

"What was it like to space from Earth to Rim before? Tell me about it. Tell me. Tell me.

"And what were the passengers like? Were all of them rich like Momma? Did . . . ?"

Candy raspberried. "A real stable orbit, that guy. But I did find out something."

What Candy found out was that no one of the current complement of the *Pequod* had been with her when she spaced some months before, bearing my old body to Rim. Crews need to be rotated regularly. Keeps them in trim. Gives the officers broader experience. Or so maintained First Officer Duncan Starbuck.

"There's the manifest and the logs from the voyage." Candy spoke in a cool, distant voice that now had little of the eleven-year-old in it. "Both are in the Captain's office safe. It's open during the workday.

"But the office is guarded by the Sergeant-at-Arms through the day. Not to mention the secretary. The First Officer and Chief Steward Inger have access to the safe. But I doubt that even little old Candy Forth could manage to maneuver Dunkie into something like that."

Candy got up and stubbed out her cigarette before she reverted to her little-girl voice.

"I'd just love to see the manifest and log for the last Earth–Rim voyage of the *Pequod*. Almost as much fun as a twenty-cartoon frizzie. Please, please, Dunkie.

"That would go over like a lead raiser in a thin atmosphere.

"And I don't think either of us would do any better with Chief Inger or the Captain. We have got to get into the safe after working hours."

Candy flopped down on my bed between my legs, her head on my belly and pale blond hairs splashed over my thighs. She looked upward at the elaborate, mildly erotic mural that covered the ceiling of the master bedroom of the suite.

"But there's a problem. I wouldn't have the slightest trouble opening the Captain's door. Simple four-gimbal lock.

"A minor problem is that we will need the Captain away from his suite. But the real catch is that Captain Brainbridge personally locks his safe at the end of the day and opens it in the morning. The problem is what keeps the safe closed. It's a *crater* lock. A crater lock. Do you know how a crater lock works? Brainbridge himself is the key, he doesn't just carry it around with him.

"Momma, I think you're going to have to be a tosser." The lumps suddenly felt very lumpy. I felt acid coming up my throat as Candy went on. "A sharp, agile professional.

"A real gusty five-thousand-credit whore."

XII

She will have to learn to be a woman. She must realize that this will be hard *and* that it can be done.

—I. F. + S. C. Operation Logbook

It is possible to admire fingers. Imagine Candy Darling, eighty going on twelve, now Candice Armitage Forth. A leggy, prepubescent blue-eyed beauty with long pale-blond hair. When she does not speak, nothing hints of anything else, except perhaps her hands. At one time or another, you've realized that the face of people over thirty reveals them. But hands tell their tales too. And often earlier in life.

Even in repose Candy's hands are surprisingly powerful. Fingers thick, proportionate to their length, like the fingers of real pianists and surgeons as opposed to those of romantic visions. Efficient tools.

When Candy is fully into her charming though spunky prepubescent role, you will suddenly see her hands. Just a little jarring. Puzzling. Then the hand will move on and the eleven-year-old will reemerge.

You won't think of a nympher. There are less than a hundred in the whole Federation, after all. Just for the very rich. And they don't make a lot of noise about it.

No, you would just feel a momentary strangeness. And then forget it.

Candy's hands are more impressive in action. Deft,

decisive, sure. Extracting the modules and transducers from panels in her baggage cases. Inserting them into the otherwise innocent though enormously versatile Horst-Leica hologrammic camera that I carried in my baggage. Building the system—"more illegal than private zombies"—into the wall so that it looked like it had always been there. All you lost was the view of two erotic cherubs.

Calibrating the instrumentation.

She had me move here, move there. Hold one uncomfortable position or another, my tail folded underneath me. Invisible.

I dressed myself for the ball in the manner of M. Windrem's famous four-character performance of the stage play *Female Man.* While I was moving about, posing for Candy's calibration, I thought of the four-face mask. Candy's. The one thing in her baggage with a history.

You got an eleven-year-old face looking up at you. But the voice cracks the whip. Candy stood at the closet door just under the Horst-Leica that obscured the cherubs. Obscured them innocuously.

"Here's a mask," she said. She turned its curious fourfold structure in her fingers.

"Here."

It smelled both musty and sweaty. The dank feel that leather has after a good space of years.

"It was given me at my disappearance party near seventy years ago. When I was sixteen. My first nymphing. It's a reproduction of the four-quadrant mask that Windrem wore in *Female Man.* Male-dominated female, female living without males, male-killing female, female being fully human—you've seen it, Patricia. Anyhow, you've seen the Rebiel film version.

"The reddish quarter. The one with the scars here. That's the killer part. The black part, over your right eye, that's the dominated female. You see the eye paint and the plastic eyebrow?"

I held the stiffening leather in my hand. A tiny fleck of the bluish eye paint crumbled off. What had the mask seen over seventy years? The eye sockets looked about right for me. Candy held it up before me.

"The left forehead—the white quarter—that's the whole human part. The female man. *Man* as the whole species.

"And the green quadrant is special for you." Candy looked up, eyes sparkling, then held mine as she finally gave me the mask.

"Virginity. Or, anyhow, malelessness.

"Wear it, Patricia," Candy said.

"Wear it, Patricia, or whoever you are. Wear it."

I took it clumsily.

"Wear it, my friend."

Candy's Peter Pan costume—green tights, fluffy, near-transparent top. Would have strained the libido of a saint. It would have thrilled committed pederasts. Little immature naps just visible. Bunlike buttocks.

I wore the mask and the white garden-party tolong. The one that M. Herbert and Candy had picked out at Rostard's.

As we entered the grand salon I saw Captain Brainbridge and First Officer Duncan Starbuck. Brainbridge's bulk and air of command identified him. And his wiry pepper-colored hair stuck out from behind his mask. He was costumed as a sea officer of three centuries back. The uniform wasn't exactly military. More likely, he was dressed as a commercial sailor. Or perhaps a pirate. His mask gave him a striking scar and beard.

It was perhaps inevitable that most of the *Pequod*'s officers should have dressed as ancient sailors like their captain. Chief Inger was one of two exceptions.

He wore a uniform. But it wasn't naval. It was more magnificent than that: white, trimmed with blue-and-gold braid. A honeybee was embroidered on the bosom. He wore no mask. His hand was thrust in the waist of the jacket. Ernest Inger was the European Emperor Napoleon. Since that ruler's name was Napoleon Bonaparte, Ernest had managed to remain a first-name person. Different status, though.

Chief Engineer Trudy Double was the other officer who did not dress as a sailor. I heard her explosive laugh. She stood against the wall of a hologram of a charming farmhouse from something like the European Middle Ages. The farmhouse looked too clean, too airy, too well proportioned, to be wholly practical or believable. It was a farmhouse for fairies and princesses. Trudy Double was talking to three characters. They were probably the Texans of the Captain's table. Two of the Texans were each dressed as some sort of bizarre reptilian creature. I learned from Captain Brainbridge that they were supposed to be something called armadillos. Actually mammals, though with a most saurian casing.

Trudy Double was costumed as some sort of hairy monster. Maybe a Vegan moully. It seemed to fit her character. She had one hairy arm draped over the shoulder of the more portly armadillo, perhaps Isa Pigg V's.

I could see that Trudy Double's familiarity annoyed Captain Brainbridge. Her laughter boomed out once more as Captain Brainbridge and First Officer Duncan approached Candy and me. Duncan, like the rest of the deck officers, was dressed like Captain Brainbridge. I would have recognized him by his ramrod back if for no other reason.

But Captain Brainbridge had more important things to do than correct a minor impropriety. Me. He wanted me. Or at least so I thought. And if he did not want me now, he would soon.

My tail itched. And the acid was in my throat again. If necessary I could chew a beta pastille for my breath. They straighten up your mouth chemistry for hours.

Brainbridge took in my fourfold mask. He wore a blue-and-white-striped pullover under his dark-blue sea jacket. And his captain's cap was without braid.

"Aye, and thou art all parts of a lady, M'lady Patricia," he said. He gave his voice an antique and husky twang. After wormhole entrance at six o'clock, the whole deck and engine crew—Captain to navigator, Duncan Starbuck to Victor Blout—had gathered in the drinking salon. It was now nine o'clock. The Captain has doubtless absorbed much. And then there was the influence of wormhole flight itself.

"Ain't she a comely lass, matey," said Captain Brainbridge, slamming Duncan on the back. Duncan nearly caromed into Candy. His neck reddened. His face must have been scarlet under his mask.

"Pardon me for the beauty that overwhelms me, M'lady," continued the implacable Brainbridge. The Captain was obviously enjoying himself.

Through the long afternoon the entire deck crew had been unavailable, closeted in the bridge and the major computer compartment. The fabric of Einsteinian space twisted into extravagant and unpredictable filaments as the *Pequod* neared the oscillating normal-space coordinates of the Canopus wormhole.

As the saintly Albert Einstein had argued two centuries ago, normal space does not allow a velocity exceeding the speed of light. You would mislead in calling this a speed limit. That might suggest the image of a traffic officer stopping speeders. As if you really could exceed the speed of light but something always slowed you.

But that is to confuse what saintly Albert said. It is

not as if there's some speeder's goal, theoretically attainable, like the runner's three-minute thirty-second mile—a goal that you wanted to reach but just couldn't. There is simply no place in normal space time for the faster-than-light. As you approach the speed of light your increase in velocity must become instead a change in the character of your vehicle. Speed changes into mass. To become close to the speed of light is to become closer to being the mass of the universe.

To exceed the speed of light is to be foreign to the universe. To be outside of it.

Wormholes are such outsiders, exceptions to the rigor of normal space. Like whirlpools. Like atomic transformations within the context of normal chemical reactions. Or like chemical reactions within the context of mechanical events like impact, friction, and acceleration.

Thus in 1934 Chandrasaker argued that a star exceeding Earth's Sun's mass by two could not exist. Thus what physicists know as Chandrasaker's Limit. Such a star, when it has exhausted its major nuclear reactions, cannot exist. It cannot exist because no Einsteinian reason could be given why such a star should not shrink to less than the dimensions of a grain of sand. No reason that it should not become inexpressibly small.

Yet Chandrasaker's view was forever paradoxical. Stars of much more than two times Earth's Sun's mass are common. And many have exhausted the nuclear fuel that allows them to battle Chandrasaker's Limit. How can they exist?

The solution is that normal space, Einsteinian space, cannot everywhere exist. A wormhole is such a state of nonexistence.

Some—most—wormholes are foul. Black. There is no exit from them into normal space time. A few exit into normal space. Thus *Pequod* could penetrate through tens of hundreds of folded light-years as a mosquito might drive its proboscis through several layers of gauze.

The first wormhole trip that humans undertook successfully was in 2025. The crew of the *Sappho* managed the hundred-light-year trip from Alpha Centauri to Beta Tau in sixteen hours of subjective time. There were four female members among *Sappho*'s seven personnel. Two ended the sixteen-hour trip pregnant. A forty-year-old male virgin, mathematically talented and impossibly shy, bunked three of the females and the other two males. The whole crew wanted to do it again.

Within a few minutes, and not a few champagne daccas, the passengers had been reduced to the amorous hilarity of the officers.

The person who perhaps most fit the hologrammic scene wore tight short pants, white hose, gold-buckle shoes, a crown, and a splendid gold-bedecked long coat. He paused in conversation with the two armadillos. Taking a pinch of powder too dark to be cocaine or triorthoamine from a silver pillbox, he snorted as genteelly as such an action allowed. I was happy that he was doubled up by his explosive sneeze. Real snuff. Authenticity only at a price.

"Let me introduce you to the Dauphin de Joinville," shouted one of the armadillos to Brainbridge and me. She was definitely Isa Pigg. And even more hilariously overbearing than usual.

The Dauphin bowed. He had on an elegant black domino mask that covered only half of his face. He was the eldest of the three IBO heirs.

The other two IBOers were close cousins. It soon became apparent what their costumes were. Or, rather, costume was. And that they were very close indeed. In several ways.

Midge Mather, that is, a svelte eighteen-year-old

with long black hair like Isobella Ion and a delightfully salacious mouth. And Bertie Mather, son of Norman Saylor Mather, a wiry, curly-haired scion to a multiple of fortunes. Even brattier than his sister and a year younger.

So entered the moose. Giggling hysterically, it walked through the impalpable hologrammic wall of the farmhouse. The head emerged magically from the sparkling white walls like a swimmer from unrippled water. Then the front legs—Bertie's—and the whole beast. The moose spoke.

"Quit bumping into my *cojones,* Midge, you pathetic little cripple. And get your paws off the merchandise."

"One more insult, Bertie baby, and you will be too loose for the most well-endowed bugger in New San Francisco. I got my Steely Dan dildo back here, you meat brain."

And so Midge Mather joined us, if not in face, at least in voice and presence.

"Velcome to ze *Petit Trianon,* my dears," said the Dauphin. "We bring you Marie Antoinette's France, *Messieurs et Mesdames*—and mooses."

"Après moi le déluge," said Victor Blout. "After me, the deluge." Suiting action to words, Blout stumbled forward, falling through several cows and a stone fence and retching into a hologrammic pig's trough that would not have held a thimble of water, let alone the evidence that Blout had already overdone it.

"I believe that it was Louis the Fourteenth who said that. And he dies in bed rather than of a severed head like Louis the Sixteenth." First Officer Duncan Starbuck had come up behind me.

He contemplated the fallen Blout, already being pulled at by a dismayed steward.

"Still, there is something to be said for the guillotine," Duncan continued, mock mournfully.

This was the first display of levity I had had from Duncan. I liked him. Straight orbit and all.

Through the long afternoon, non-normal Holmann-orbit projections had relentlessly succeeded one another on the giant main screen of the major computer compartment. The bridge had a much smaller version of the same projections. Candy and I watched the navigation staff from a glassed-in gallery. Seven consoles in a semicircle were below us.

"Alpha vector one-oh-oh-five."

"Zero graphing on normal space, still."

"Watch out. Bearing scantion tau-irrational radical seven-four-oh-nine-nine is better. It's foul down the other way."

Duncan explained at the ball that wormhole entry is a little like paddling a canoe through rapids. You jockey, back-paddling, calculating, holding, until you see your opening between the white-watered rocks. Then you let go with all you've got.

Except that you spend hours calculating, and you have only one go. And if you fail you don't get wet. You just aren't anything anywhere anymore.

Finally there was a mild but authoritative cough.

"Done," pronounced the elegant, cool, high-pitched voice of Chief Navigator Arabella Q. Queeg.

She had driven the *Pequod* into the wormhole like a spear.

At fifteen the Chief Navigator had established the first humanly surveyable proof of the claim that four tints suffice to give distinct colors to every possible partitioning of a map. In 1977 a computer at the University of Illinois had examined the over three thousand special cases of the four-color problem. A human mathematician would have taken much more than an entire lifetime simply to read through a single one of these computer surveys. And so topology stood until Arabella Q. Queeg. Her proof occupied twenty-five pages of *Mathematische Studien.* It was also etched on a two-meter square sheet of platinum next to the five-hundred-year-old door to Sir Isaac Newton's rooms at Trinity College of Cambridge University.

Navigator Arabella Queeg was a native of Vega and red as a scarlet woodpecker. She played hyper-Nim with the central computer. And she talked to her Vegan Siamese cat. Once she was thought to have smiled at Third Officer Stub. But this was probably just absent-mindedness.

She did not attend the ball.

XIII

Austin Worms suggested that sexuality would be an extraordinary experience for the patient. She will have been on both sides of the masks of gender.

—I. F. + S. C. Operation Logbook

Why had I felt so giddy when Duncan's hand brushed against the back of my tolong? Perhaps part of it was that he would have felt my tail if he pressed at all hard. Brainbridge's hands were much more forward. It was not much later than twenty-three hundred hours and his hands had twice hovered over my breasts like bees over clover. They buzzed about and darted in for the sweet stuff. Rostard's impeccable tailoring had made the white tolong more austere than racy. It did, however, bare my breasts. The sense of austerity slipped more when Brainbridge made like a human brassiere with two thick hands. The trick now was to balance him. I had to keep him hot but away from below my bellybutton until I got him back to my stateroom. Or at least until he was so wiped that he wouldn't recognize what was wrapped around my waist under the puffed structure of the tolong.

Say, this was fun.

My breasts no longer felt like dead lumps. I was aware of their firm, small appearance. The nipples stood up like two ripe olives. The aureoles felt, oh, congested and lively. Perhaps from the cool air, yes. And people's eyes. And of course the Captain's hands.

"Momma's little apples" was what Candy had said when I had put the tolong on in our stateroom.

I would have to remember to think of the Captain as Mathew. Matt. I would have to.

The moose now stood between two cows, its backside and rear legs obscured by a hologrammic statue of young Octavius Caesar. I did not think that Midge knew she was troubling the illusion of the *Petit Trianon,* however. Bertie certainly didn't.

The front legs of the moose were shaking rhythmically, faster and faster. You could hear Bertie's pants. I don't know whether Midge's rumored Steely Dan was in operation. But the chest of the moose was being buffeted in and out between its front legs.

"The moose looks like it is going to have a heart attack, don't you think?" I said, smiling at Duncan.

The First Officer choked on his laugh. I could see his blue eyes through the openings in his mask. His pupils were dilated.

Bertie gave a final *whoosh.* The front half of the moose fell forward. Midge's face and forearms, and the back half of the moose, emerged from the shining white statue of the father of the Roman Empire.

"Imperial decadence," said Duncan.

"Your turn in back, Bertie," said Midge.

"My baton, Maestro," said Bertie, emerging from the crumpled foresection of the moose. He grabbed the Steely Dan from Midge's left hand.

Candy, Candy, Candy, how can I do this? How can I stand this? The man is drunk, yes. The man is crazy over what he imagines as my zenith class. That really means my money, my clothes, my breeding. Yet my clothes will have to go when he has me on that bed. And you can't wear money there, either.

Breeding? I'm just—I was just—an ordinary guy. Sally Forth was a prospector, a tramp of space. Her body was straight and wiry strong, her face, my face, high cheekboned, taut chin lines. We.

Are.

For it.

How we loved weightlessness. How I love?

Toilets can be a problem when you have a tail. Particularly if you're hiding it. And—ah—the release of letting it out. Letting it free. The questing, inquisitive feel of the tip, like some incredible prolongation of my spine into the grip of a couple of powerful fingers—and the flexibility and sensitivity of a tongue. And the pleasing heft of the main body of my tail.

I pulled the tolong up to my bellybutton. Held it there with the upper part of my arms while I slid the gossamer tights down my thighs. Gossamer woven from the web filaments of the undomesticable moon spiders of Vega's second planet. Strong. Also used for sutures in inner-ear surgery. The packaging, M. Herbert, the packaging is superb. But what of the contents?

Or am I perhaps an onion, all peelings and no core? All surface, no inside or outside, like a Klein bottle? And I imagine an inner voice that says, After the first death there is no other. No other, other.

"Remember two things, Momma," Candy whispered in my ear before she went, dutiful child, to our stateroom, Chief Steward Inger looking hungrily after her, one of his Napoleonic golden bees bedecked with the tears of some complicated emotion.

"Remember. If . . . no, *when* the clothes come off, you need merely lie back and let it happen. Remember that he's eager, drunk, and bemused at rutting with a zenith-class lady. Probably already thinking about telling some buddy about it. And he'll follow your lead in anything because everyone who isn't zenith class thinks zenith-class sex is kinky and sophisticated. And they don't want to blow it.

"Remember that no man can be overflattered about his sexual performance.

"And remember that only half of you is a virgin."

Those strong, fine hands held me momentarily, and I looked down at Peter Pan's green mask.

"And remember what Germaine Means said. A tail is not a sexual organ. A tail is a tool, a sensor. More a pen than a penis, more an eye than a gut."

I felt the urine sluice between my legs. More of a hissing sound than before. And no loud tinkling of the drops against the porcelain.

Looking down, I parted my pinkish lips. I could see two drops of urine glistening among the hairs like dew in a ground spider's web. I smoothed my thumbs down the pen-nib-sized organ. So like the erect penis of a small male cat. Maybe we are all the same, only distorted in various ways. Like what you see in the mirrors of fun houses.

I felt the queasiness and inner contortions that I had with my first period. I once could press four hundred pounds. I'm weak, small, female.

I was startled to realize that urine smelled like perfume.

It's so small, so small. My questing middle finger moved more easily than ever before. My flesh inside was plumper. Slippery. I am only half a virgin. Or less.

Candy, Candy, Candy. How?

"You're like a whale," I whispered as he entered me with difficulty. Indeed he had all the grace of a beached whale as he lay there on top of me. But I do not think that he thought I was referring to the whole of his anatomy.

First he wallowed on me for five minutes, then he entered me again. Slob. I had to keep him in position for at least twenty minutes. I used my fingers on his arse when his erection faltered again. He was so heavy.

A cherub's face turned into Candy above me. She smiled down at the primal scene. Then four fingers. Four minutes more at least. Candy waved. She returned to her invisible maneuvers behind the Horst-Leica.

"Matt," I breathed. "Matt, my Captain." Our fateful trip is almost done, I hope.

I knew that I got more from Candy's hands as they briefly held me before she left the ball than from all of Brainbridge's gropings. Even dear, shy Duncan's hand against the back of my tolong had been more sensual.

Gropings. Pinchings. Squeezings. As if my breasts were lemons and his hands robot juicers. His movements had become more shaky, more crude after the first few minutes on top of me. Spreading my legs as if they were logs. Gruntings. Grunting as he tried to pinch my breasts while keeping his chest up. Spitting in my ear (doubtless he meant to blow gently, but he was drunk and careless and piggish).

"Stay on my saddle, you brute," I said the one time he had the grace to suggest a change of position. By the puffs, that remark seemed to please him almost as much as the one about the whale.

I had to keep him on top for twenty minutes. Candy needed that time to make a simulation of the crater lock. Captain Brainbridge himself was the crater-lock key.

A crater lock is tuned to open only to the neurological pattern of the five-thousand-odd neurochemically active lattices of the nerves within one person's spinal column. In practical terms the crater pattern is several hundred times more unique than finger or retinal prints. And it changes and must be reset every month or so. And best of all, from security's viewpoint, it is very difficult to simulate. With the best sort of licensed and radon-alpha-sealed equipment, you needed about fifteen minutes to get a good simulation, according to Candy. Only a few people knew it was possible. "You and only you are the key" was the publicly undisputed claim of Crater Lock INP.

After Candy had left the ball and I returned from the toilet, I had found Captain Brainbridge and Trudy Double arm-wrestling. The Captain's antique sailor rig and the Chief Engineer's hairy monster costume made a fetching contrast. For a space of a minute or so they sat facing, hand against hand, like some tableau of man and beast, technology and jungle, mind and matter. Finally, the Captain's superior weight told.

I had been glad that Captain Brainbridge had won. A defeated man is a suspicious man. He stretched, straightening his shoulders.

"Your muscles are stiff, I imagine," I said. I reached both hands over his shoulders, stroking my thumbs over the muscles between his shoulder blades and spine. My touch was firm but with the slightest overtone of a caress.

"I don't suppose you'll allow me a rematch in the squid race, Captain?" asked Chief Double. Her laugh was like a bark. She was too tall and lean to be a very animal-looking monster. Impressive, though.

"No, matey," said Captain Brainbridge. He was maintaining his antique voice. "Ye'll hardly catch me in that sort of space-larking, a bearded gentleman such as meself.

"Besides," he added, giving a glance down at my breasts, "I have a most distinguished lady at my side."

I had looked up at him. The fourfold mask I wore concealed my expression. He had nothing to go on but my expressionless eyes, my lips, and the prejudiced voice of his libido.

"Perhaps," I said as the Chief Engineer and the others turned away, "perhaps you would find a back rub some comfort. I am not untalented as a masseuse."

My fingers slipped to his buttocks, taut within the blue wide-bottomed pants. "I find it so bourgeois when a woman lacks the basic skills of the boudoir."

I had him harpooned. He saw only me. Felt only my fingers between his legs.

"I have a *recherché* massage oil in my stateroom. Orlando Pons. From Rostard's of Houston. A superior tingle.

"Come with me, Mathew. Matt.

"I always have a good wine in my ice bucket. And there's some commendable Vegan leaf." It would serve Candy right if the Captain went for that.

"Come."

I had led him away. His eyes had looked glazed. He had looked to be a very happy man.

Behind us the noise of various officers' squid-race challenges. One of the armadillos was bare from the waist down. He was bare because he had been trying to spell ALAMO on a bulkhead. His aim was doubtless affected by the changes that were occurring in the holograms. The Versailles of Louis XVI was changing into the Washington Square Park of New York City in the 1960's. Raucous music had been replacing the Vivaldi. Seven of the revelers disappeared from view inside a gigantic hologram of Washington Square Arch. The Dauphin de Joinville was embarrassing an ostrich.

The Captain did not know that the massage oil was impregnated with a complex of magnotransducing rare earths that would make it possible for Candy to simulate the crater key.

As we had left I had heard one of the mates stage-whisper to Chief Engineer Double: "Captain can't squid race better than a groundhog, but he gets his share." What was a squid race?

After I had worked his muscles and thoroughly covered his back with the ersatz Orlando Pons oil, I stood back from the goatish and thoroughly bemused Brainbridge. He had removed his mask as he entered my stateroom. His large baby-fat face was flushed. The rare earths were in his skin, invisible.

"Why don't you use the fresher, Captain, while I mix up something interesting? Don't bother putting your clothes back on." When I heard the water running, I had dimmed the lights, pulled off my shoes, mask, tolong, and tights. Candy was already in position, concealed by a hologrammic projection that lowered the spacious ceiling by two feet.

I lay naked, waiting, tail concealed beneath me in the bedclothes.

"Come to me," I had said when he returned.

While he puffed I saw the fourfold mask, just barely visible in dim light, looking at me from where I had hung it.

After Candy signaled and Brainbridge the whale came, legs spasming between mine, I once again suggested the fresher. This time around a gadget of Candy's would feed a chemical into the spray that would remove the rare-earth traces.

"Go, love, have your shower. Let me enjoy your sperm dripping between my thighs."

Actually, I wasn't the inventor of that line. I was having trouble figuring out how to get him out of the room and into the shower without revealing my tail. Suddenly the words appeared on the ceiling like a message from the gods. Candy, seeing my difficulty, had projected it up there. It was all I could do to stop myself from laughing, or retching.

But Candy's line worked like a charm. He sang in the shower. I put a heavy silk robe on, wrapping my poor tail once more around me. We will exercise tomorrow, I said to it.

I would have felt drained and wretched for the rest of the night except for what Captain Brainbridge pointed out when he returned once more from the fresher.

"Chief's the only officer I've ever known like that," he said. For the first time in several hours he seemed interested in something other than my body. He stood looking out of my stateroom view port. I saw that he was looking down the two-hundred-meter-long tube that connected the globular power section of *Pequod* with the similarly shaped command and passenger section that contained us. And then I saw it. Flashing crazily as one or another view port or running lamp illumed its mad, gay progress.

Dumbbell-shaped, *Pequod* simulated gravity by rotating around an axis running down its length. This provides weight, particularly as one approaches the portions of both globes that are farthest from the axis. But the connecting tube itself and portions of it running into both globes have weightlessness. A squid race is a race through or along this weightless tube, from power section to command. It is called a squid race because of the mode of travel an experienced spacer uses to race in weightlessness. Running is impossible, of course, and neither vacuum nor air provides enough resistance for paddling. You grab things, you pull yourself along in a squidlike manner by hand, throwing your body forward feet first. Then while flying forward, you flip yourself so that your hands are again in front. ready to grab and pull once more. Mad tumbling in space, or through the tube corridor.

Or at least something like that was Captain Brainbridge's explanation. I wasn't listening much, transfigured by what I saw out of the view port.

It was Chief Engineer Trudy Double. In weightlessness, like some sort of supermonkey, she was swinging from mast to antenna to disc to handhold or what all, ripping along from the power section to my own. But Trudy Double didn't have to flip herself around after throwing herself forward feet first with her hands. No, when she was zipping forward feet first she would grab from between them with a tail. Her tail. And then forcefully swing herself forward by her tail, now becoming hand first once again. Imagine the most beautiful, most exciting high-wire circus aerial flips you've ever seen. Make the flips bigger, more graceful, and have them happen again, and again, and unbelievably again. Space larking.

My tail felt electric.

"You didn't think the tail to her gorilla suit was a fake, did you?" said Captain Brainbridge. He seemed puzzled by my complete bewitchment with the scene.

"It's not much of a race, you know," he added. "She always wins. Even though she does the double course, here to there and then back again."

At last Brainbridge was gone. And Candy was off to burgle the crater safe. Wormhole festivity night was the safest time to do that job. Most of the crew were drunk, amorously entwined, or both. My tail still felt electric as I remembered the race of Chief Engineer Trudy Double. Slack time. Own time.

I put the fourfold mask on once more.

I found Duncan Starbuck, Chief Inger, Trudy Double, Victor Blout, and Officer Stubb singing one of the mournful space chanties out of New Scotland

You could not see below their waists. They were obscured by the concrete and water of a large fountain. Though thus properly situated for the part, they hardly looked or sounded like Rhine maidens.

"Duncan," I said at the end of one particularly lugubrious stanza. The song had begun, "Annie spaced from Triton and her hair was deep-space black." Things got worse and worse after that, death succeeding death, including, in merciless specificity, the families of both Annie and the singer, plus the singer's space bat, Annie's dog, Hardtack, and a cow whose ownership seemed to be in doubt. And Annie herself, of course, wasted into decorously pale doom by nothing more clear than grief and loneliness—or, perhaps, boredom.

"Duncan?"

"My lady, my lady," he said, first thickly, then courtly, as one who wakes.

"Duncan, come here. I have something to show you."

Candy would hate me for this.

But I was sick of stealth and sick of deception.

When I uncovered he stared at my tail. And then with enormous seriousness he bent and kissed it from tip to arse.

"You will say nothing of it."

I am whale, I am whale. Sweeping through me, over and over. I am raiser, I am packet. *Gxxhdt Gxxhdt,* Again. Mmm. From tail tip to toe tingle, from gracious finger to greedy mouth, from haunch to heart, past Eve and Adam, from swerve of hip to bend of thigh, from tail to tale, past Duncan's castle and oh-so-tiny olives, hair and skin encased, till thousandsee, till chloroplast and sunlight make life, till all the Earth sends up grasses. Again. Mmm.

Returning from Duncan's suite I passed Brainbridge's office. Hope Candy got something. CAPTAIN MATHEW AHAB BRAINBRIDGE, COMMANDING was what the billet plaque said. "Got you" was what I said.

I was drifting off to sleep at five, spent. In a few hours *Pequod* would reenter normal space, without much more ado than a cork released under water might make in reaching the surface. The problem was getting in right. Getting out took care of itself.

In moving about above, Candy had displaced a mini-spot that had illumed the cherubs and lovers of the ceiling. Now the light shone down and from behind the mask. I had put the mask over the top of the open wardrobe door. And the air system must have just kicked in because the mask was swaying. Swaying so that the light coming through the eye sockets waxed and waned. As if the eyes were moving, peering.

The black-and-green quarters of the mask's right half seemed to bleed together and separate, again and again. The black forehead was the dominated woman. The green cheek and jaw was the maleless woman. You could read in it that I had lost my virginity and that I had been male-dominated. Male-dominated, the whale atop spuming in my ear.

Yet I had manipulated Captain Brainbridge. I had used, though not in the way that he had used. In a way I had won. When I was Ismael Forth I had sometimes felt contempt at premodern women, at housewives, and at house husbands for that matter. An easy ride, Ismael Forth had thought.

But then, why had I felt filthy after my session with Brainbridge? Why had I felt I had lost? Lost.

And then I understood in my guts something Dr. Germaine Means had said, seemingly so long ago. I felt company with every dominated person, every adult made child, secretary, servant, lackey, cur, chattel, plaything, slave, possession. Our only victories are always defeats, always reassertions of our status. Cunning, cousining, suckling up to. Manipulating someone because one cannot straightforwardly ask, demand, earn, or take for oneself.

"In premodern society women were not regular members of the armed forces. They were not allowed to fight. As late as the twentieth century you would find males saying that females had it soft because they were not inducted into the vast armies of the time. There are still a few males like that today. What they ignore is obvious. No slave society ever allowed its slaves to bear arms. No really racist society ever allowed many of the racially dominated group to be full-fledged soldiers. Soft is very hard indeed."

That was what Germaine Means had said. I thought of the blood-red lower lefthand quadrant of the mask. It was mostly in darkness. The killer, the slave rebellion, Spartacus. Could I kill? Would I?

I remembered when Uncle Herbert had taken me to a friend's quaint antiquarian farm in Williamsburg. He showed me how a chicken was slaughtered. Some of the blood that spurted from the animal's neck had hit my hand. I washed it for hours. I didn't eat chicken for a long time after that. Squeamish. And I loved eating chicken.

"You ought to be able to kill what you want" was what Uncle Herbert said.

Would I be the whole mask, black, green, red, white? The white of full humanness, holding it all together?

Candy hadn't been angry that I had bedded Duncan. She chuckled at me, holding the copies she had made of the ship's files.

"Good for you, Patricia. Bet you popped the socks off him." She gave me an unchildish kiss.

"Maybe we ought to try a Vegan sandwich with a couple of guys sometime" was the last thing she said that night. Her laugh was easy and friendly. The mask continued to blink at me as I disappeared into sleep. Perhaps it was laughing too.

Rim awaited us.

XIV

I have seen François Vase lose his temper only once. When I made a joke about Philpritz Modulation. I replied that a collector of Aubrey Beardsley and S. Clay Wilson had no right to be so sensitive, but . . .

—I. F. + S. C. Operation Logbook, Append. I, Dossiers

"It's a Philpritz Modulator," said Candy.

She was surrounded by reproductions of *Pequod's* papers dating from the voyage that had taken my old body to Rim. She wasn't speaking to me. Her voice was a whisper with a strange tension in it. I could see her staring at a photograph. Her hand had reached up to the back of her neck, the fingers slowly, absently stroking her spine. I could see her face now in the mirror covering the wardrobe door.

Fear. That was it. Fear, horror, something like that. And a grim tension in the cheek muscles. I had never seen anything like that in Candy's face before.

Her free hand stroked down from her forehead, shutting her own eyes. A slow full breath in, a pause, then a measured exhalation with just a touch of tremor in it. She stayed like that for perhaps a minute: legs folded under, one hand over her eyes, the other covering her neck.

Then she rubbed her eyes and put her hands to her side. Her eyes were cold.

"Do you know what a thumbscrew is?" she asked quietly and clearly.

"No," I said. "And I don't know what a Philpritz Modulator is, either."

She turned and looked me up and down. Then she turned back again and began to speak slowly and monotonously and precisely. She turned away, as if she did not wish to see a human being while she spoke.

"Seventy years ago, when I was really eleven or so, I read United States history. Congressional history. The projectile-handgun-control debates of the 2000's. A congressperson said that just as a thumbscrew, a projectile handgun had nothing but an evil use. It had no other earthly purpose but killing humans.

"Someone on the other side said that that comparison wasn't right. Killing was sometimes justified. In self-defense. In killing to save other lives. But a thumbscrew was always wrong to use. *Intrinsically* wrong, he said.

"I looked up the word 'intrinsically.' I found out what that meant. But I couldn't find 'thumbscrew' in the dictionary. I was curious. What could be worse than a device for killing people? So I read around and found out what a thumbscrew was.

"It's a very simple mechanical device. Imagine a hollow with three internal surfaces. A fourth surface can be moved in or out of the hollow with great force and slowness by a mechanical screw. The interior surface may be smooth but is more likely ribbed or studded. Like a simple woodworking vise except that it is fit for no other purpose than grasping the human thumb or finger. Grasping and gradually crushing, breaking, grinding . . ."

I wanted to go away then. But the cold, even voice held me stock-still.

"Physical torture. The attempt to extract a confession or information, or just to torment, through specialized instruments.

"And there were others. I wangled an adult media card and read ancient history, read and read. Leg screws, racks, iron maidens, the thousand cuts, the strappado, pincers, the boot, hot coals, boiling water, ants, rats, the stake."

Her voice was still cold and even. Crazy. The eyes open, staring. And blue and empty, like a clear Earth sky.

"I once tried to explain physical torture to a Regilian. Oh, it wasn't back then in 2052 when I first read this stuff, before we ran into the Regilian octopoids. It was just five years ago. We talked about literature. About Dylan Thomas and Xenophon, and Storba. Drinking dacca, which affects them just like us.

"Trylig couldn't understand what I meant. Just couldn't understand the concept of deliberate physical torture. I don't mean wouldn't accept. Trylig couldn't grasp it."

The voice was still cold and even, a clear soprano. Three drops eased slowly down Candy's left eye.

"We drank dacca and I smoked Vegan and we played pisque and held each other, that Regilian and me. He liked my size. But Trylig never understood, Sol bless it, her, him, or whatever. Trylig never understood."

There was a long pause. I brought Candy her fixings. When she fumbled I reached for the papers and leaf. She gave me one look and I backed off. Her movements became precise.

"Of course, the projectile-gun-control congressperson had a response. If you can kill to save people's lives, if that can justify the projectile handgun, then why not the thumbscrew? Why not the thumbscrew to gain information to save lives? Why not? Why not the boot and the strappado, the rack, the eye pincers? Why not a Philpritz Modulator to accomplish some noble purpose?"

Candy shook her head and looked, finally, directly at me. She handed me the photograph she had stared at.

"A log entry, theoretically—photos at the end that the logperson hadn't had a chance to index. They missed it. Didn't know shipboard procedures."

Candy handed me the magnifying glass. There was someone, backside up, lying on one of the *Pequod*'s bunks. Sprawled in a slack and disorderly way.

Candy pointed, under the glass, to a ridge above his neck. And to the squarish shadow against the bulkhead over his shoulder.

"The Philpritz Modulator fits over the back of your neck. There. It has no other use than the domination of a human body and a human mind. No other use whatsoever. Possession or manufacture of a Philpritz Modulator is grounds for permanent incarceration or mind-alteration therapy. But if some psycheticians got ahold of you first, it could be much worse. Vampires take care of their own."

Then, of course, I realized why the body was eerily familiar. Ismael Forth.

I was now on the floor next to Candy. I was conscious that some of the muscles in my left cheek were spasming. I did not know when I got down. I was there for some minutes. I felt Candy's hands on me briefly. She cleared her throat and went on, firmly, efficiently. Pulling me into things once more.

Candy flipped some ordinary typed log pages in front of me. She handed me the magnifier again.

"See that edge over there. And look at the log page numbers. Clever, but not good enough. I caught myself when I was photographing. You can see the irregularity if you flip the log pages over quickly. The numbers on those pages are slightly displaced. They probably took them from another blank logbook.

"Two pages of *Pequod*'s log were removed. And the crew was reassigned to a stint that would take them far from this part of the galaxy. That means real influence."

I didn't understand what had happened. I told Candy so.

"Oh, it's not difficult to figure out the essentials," continued Candy. "The rest of the log is normal. The crew and passengers didn't realize anything. Except, of course, whoever was minding the Ismael Forth body.

"You can see the initials of the medical orderly on the edge of the photograph. The Ismael Forth body must have had a minor seizure or something. And in public, or maybe when a steward went in the stateroom by accident.

"So the ship's doctor would have been called, and part of the routine would have been to take a photograph. All that would have stopped quick and smooth, though, or they would have noticed the Philpritz Modulator. Not necessarily recognized what it was, but enough to make them puzzle and ask questions that would need real answers.

"There's a passenger listed as bunking next to Ismael Forth, a Delbert Sperling, M.D. He must have been minding Ismael Forth. Must have shooed the ship's personnel out. But there still would have been a log entry, and at least three or four of the *Pequod*'s staff would have memories of a minor incident.

"So the log had to be changed and the *Pequod*'s personnel sent as far away as possible. Rotation is common enough but it's almost always partial. This time they all went."

Candy looked at me. She took a final drag on her Vegan, squashed it, and began shoveling the papers together. Packing, sorting, clearing up, and making unsuspicious.

"Patty, m'dear," she said several minutes later, "we are dealing with some very big and very careful people."

We had come out of the wormhole that morning,

emerging with plenty of Rim-ward velocity no more than a few light-minutes from our destination. We were due to rendezvous with Rim's packet boat at eleven hundred hours tomorrow.

Bad dreams that night. Endless weary walking. Germaine Means and Austin Worms chasing me through the corridors of NWRH. My old body, looming up out of the darkness. I saw some device in its hands. I ran. Endless, fearful fragments.

When I awoke in my sweat-damp bed it was but six hundred hours. The first thing I saw was Candy Darling. She must have heard me in the night. She was asleep in the armchair that she must have pulled next to my bunk. Her so-innocent-looking head lolled against the back of the chair.

She had composed a coded message—ostensibly from Lady Patricia Forth—that would go out by hyper-F, duplicates by regulation going into the ship's transmission records and to the local Federation office on Rim.

But we were going into Rim alone. I could hear Candy's even breathing. How was it that I was no longer afraid?

XV

The older harmonizers whisper the story that Candy Darling and a psychetician were accused of killing someone some forty years ago. While I am not free to verify this, my own feeling is that if Candy Darling killed someone, he deserved it.

—I. F. + S. C. Operation Logbook,
Append. I, Dossiers

"Well, I wrote we should go north," said Candy, folding up the pilot's relief map. "We'll just be going farther north than we'd planned on."

Her face was grimy from the smoke. There was a large black smear of graphite lubricant on her forehead where she had pushed back her hair. The front of her classic white dress was splattered with some sort of greenish chemical from the instrument panel.

The air was full of the smell of burning things. The thick oily stench of the flame-resistant seat padding, which was turning to a viscous liquid in the heat. The breath-catching smell of insulator plastics, transistors, batteries, ernoids, and silicones in the smoldering instrument panel. The acrid, nutty, evil smell of our scorched hair and his burned flesh.

"Quick," she said, "put the emergency pack on." She pushed my unresisting arms through the straps and slipped the light pack up on my back. I was dazed.

"March, damn you. Go for those trees up that way. Quick. They'll be here in a few minutes and they'll kill us. What's two more to them?"

Still dazed, I turned to the mangled helicopter. One rotor blade and its tail in the air, it looked like some monstrous black insect. Fire crackled in the control and passenger areas. Flame had not got to the shiny fuel tanks slung under the fuselage.

"March, Patty, and forget Mr. Jacobs. His whole chest was wiped by the laser blast that hit the controls. Who do you think is all over your front?"

I looked down at my gray tolong. There was one great splash of blood across my left breast. And a piece of half-seared flesh was caught in the medallion. The laser had sliced his chest strap too. His broken torso had swung over on me.

"I got things to do. Now get. Double time to the trees up there. Upcountry." She pushed me from behind. I got. A couple of hundred meters off to my right I could see yet another one of those giant signs that said, in letters large enough to read from the sky,

DANGER—NO ENTRY
ECOLOGICALLY RESTRICTED AREA

We had crossed the first series of them at least ten kilometers back. I wondered why they bothered putting one this far in. Anyone close enough to read it from their flier would already be in the firing range of the automatic track-and-fire laser rifle that had brought us down.

Officially, the packet boat had glided us into Xanadu, Rim's only town. In fact, everyone called it Rim City. "City" was a trifle of an exaggeration. There was the Xanadu Hilton Lodge, Rim Port, a small Federation office, a marina two kilometers south on Lake Mather, and a handful of small buildings. There was also the rumored Executive Eyrie, some kilometers north up the one permitted corridor into the ecologically restricted forest lands.

Discovered some thirty years ago, Rim was of Earth mass but clear of humans aside from the hunting and lake area stretching in an arc some one hundred and fifty kilometers south of Rim City. The Rim City area was a tiny portion of the mideast of a sprawling northern continent that covered more than half the globe from east to west. Federation surveyors and biologists had laid out the visual grid of sixty-odd automatic video posts over the northern and two southern continents. But since that time humans had been restricted by law to an area not much larger than Earth's island of Hawaii. The Rim City climate was mild. And it was mild through the year, for Rim varied less than Earth in orbital inclination as it circled its sun. You could have snow fall a few hundred kilometers north. But not around Rim City.

The select guests of the Xanadu Hilton Lodge hunted terran moose in the open area south of Rim City. They fished Lake Mather. Or they cast flies for the hybrid trout in the streams leading into Lake Mather.

And they had the glories of the Xanadu Lodge itself. French and Vegan cuisine. Total dimensional private-booth frizzies. An inevitably vulgar but quite convincing reproduction of the nineteenth-century Hotel Monaco gambling hall. And small but zenith-class health and sexual accommodations.

There were rooms for no more than sixty guests at the Xanadu Hilton. That should mean, and probably did, at least three hundred lodge personnel. I remembered a line from Isobella Beeton's *Zenith-Class Life:* "Even with the most judicious employment of modern technology it is a received maxim that it is necessary to maintain a ratio of five servitors to every person."

Candy had managed to draw out the elderly manager of the marina on the first day. It appeared that the Executive Eyrie had perhaps threescore personnel and, for the moment, no more than a half-dozen guests. Midge and Bertie had apparently gone up there. They were the only Pequodians aside from the Piggs to land on Rim.

Add to that the twenty or so Federation and raiser-port personnel and some fishing and hunting guides, and you have a little less than five hundred people. Not much for even the twenty-thousand-odd square kilometers around Rim City that were ecologically accessible to humans.

"You could hide anything here" was what Candy had said when we got back to our room at the end of our first day on Rim. Candy was laid out flat on her bed. We had just returned from a talk with the marina people and a long walk around the Rim City area. Before that Candy had talked in confidence with the two Federation officers about Ismael Forth's drowning. I'd snooped around the Xanadu Lodge to no effect.

If anything I'd felt more tired than Candy when we got to our room. She was in great physical shape. But instead of lying down, I paced around nervously.

"Funny that they should have got permission for this size of ecological violation but no larger," said Candy. "You could have a million people here without much more damage. And if you wanted to keep it untouched, why allow this? Plus Earth-import moose and hybrid trout. IBO must have used megapull on this one. They . . ."

Candy was watching me. I stopped pacing. The room had not made me feel uncomfortable before. I stripped off my dress and let my tail loose. That would make me comfortable.

It didn't.

Candy motioned me to walk around. I realized my tail was tingling as it had at Rostard's of Houston. I felt annoyed that Candy had realized what was going on before I did. Candy put her finger to her lips when I turned to her.

"That's what they all say about IBO around here.

Lotsa money. And they can give your hair a full alpha-lux treatment. Couldn't get that on the *Pequod,* and . . ." Candy continued chattering while she watched me. A couple of times she moved so that I would cover a particular area.

We found it soon enough. Built into the top of a light fixture, it scanned the sitting room and most of one bedroom. Candy took a careful look at it. It didn't look like that was what she was doing. She was apparently deciding where and how to hang a picture of Randy Krupa, the electric vroomist.

And then we decided to write letters. Candy showed me the one she wrote to Uncle Tinsley. It was for me, of course. "Hurried installation, not very professional," I read. "It's got visual and auditory function. They put it in while we were out today. Ismael Forth was supposed to have drowned in a diving accident south of here in the middle of Lake Mather. South—where they wouldn't mind people looking, I bet. We'll rent a view-copter and go north tomorrow. Don't say anything about it now. It'll be a sudden whim."

As I read her note Candy had continued to chatter. She was good at it. I contented myself with an occasional abstracted "Yes, my dear."

Early the next day we rented a helicopter from Xanadu Hunting and Touring. Mr. Jacobs, our pilot, was a lanky, easy-going man in his forties. He was happy to view-copter an aristocratic young woman and her coltish eleven-year-old daughter. He was less happy later.

We began with a leisurely sweep to the southwest. To the north we could see the line of ecological restriction signs that indicated prohibited territory. A few kilometers out of Rim City I had begun to hint at an interest in taking a look north. There were some mountains up there. Innocent and charming Candy took up the appeal.

The mountains were too far. And it was illegal.

Well, we just wanted a glimpse. Money was no object among friends. Mommy was a big tipper (that last from Candy in a whisper).

It was illegal and they were real tough on things like that. He could lose his contract.

Patricia Cabot Forth did not forget someone who did a favor, someone who was a friend. Why, once on Vega, a loutish maître d' had actually fired a waiter who had made sure that the Forth table got the last of the fresh *glenna un petit*. The next day the waiter became manager of an exclusive restaurant. And the day after that the maître d' found himself unemployed and unemployable. And so on.

We seemed to have come close to getting Mr. Jacobs' help when I mentioned a particular interest in flying up north of the Executive Eyrie. That made Mr. Jacobs look particularly worried. And adamantine about his refusal to help. Candy pointed at him. Jacobs appealed to her. Even such an innocent, charming young girl had to understand . . .

We did not learn what Candy had to understand. Mr. Jacobs had slumped forward into his seat harness, a glassy look in his now half-open eyes. Candy took the controls in an efficient and confident way.

"You'll find some philex in the medkit just back of your seat," said Candy. "Wipe his throat and put just a dab of the philex on it. No marks by the time we get back."

I found two drops of blood and a small puncture to the left of Jacobs' Adam's apple. They disappeared.

"I'll put him to on the way back. Just confront him with what we've done. They'll never believe that he was just a victim. Better take our money and chance getting away with it. And so on."

Candy had grinned at me across the inert body.

"North. Upcountry."

We soared up north through the signs that strictly

prohibited such travel. Ecological-restriction signs. We had skirted a cleared area a few kilometers north of Rim City. Probably the Executive Eyrie. Some twenty kilometers north of Rim City we found out that the prohibition had more force behind it than signs. And we found out why.

North of Rim City you find a mottling of grass and scrub land and forest. Small hills and valleys.

Candy kept the helicopter low as we crisscrossed northward. I scanned with low-power vibration-stabilized binoculars. But it was Candy who saw them first as we came over the lip of a small valley.

"Zombies," she said. She grabbed the binoculars and thrust the control stick in my hand. "Just keep her steady."

I could see the group of young males. They were doing what looked like calisthenics in a large cleared area. A fully dressed figure directed them.

"Yeah, zombies. I bet those are Philpritz Modulators," said Candy. "Let's get down and out of here."

And then the laser hit, and Mr. Jacobs was dead, and we were on the ground on an upland plain a kilometer or two north of an exercise field for zombies. Not blanked-mind bodies in research hospitals. No, real people, with real minds under Philpritz Modulator control. Spare parts.

I marched toward the tree line automatically. This was my first time with sudden death. I made no effort to wipe the blood from the front of my tolong. It would have done no good. I could feel the dampness soaking through. I picked the piece of flesh out of the medallion. One had to be careful about how one walked.

I was three-fourths of the way to the trees when I was hit by the explosive *whoomp-whoomp* of the fuel tanks. Candy must have set them off. I saw her pop up from some sheltering rocks near the inferno. She ran toward me. When we reached the tree line a few minutes later, Candy had her plans formed.

There was a reasonable chance they might think we all died in the crash. The heat from two acetylnovine tanks would leave practically nothing of Jacobs' body. What was left could be confused into three bodies.

Going south toward Rim was out. We had seen zombies. We had been hit by a device which was nearly as illegal as zombies themselves. Under no conditions could we be allowed to get to Rim City. Under no conditions could we be allowed to live. So north was the hope. Upcountry.

"We have the pilot's local map, a tourist map of Rim, and a survival pack" was what Candy said as we reached the cover of the trees. She pointed on the tourist map to an intersection north of Rim City.

"It's an automatic video tracking post. Federation, like the other sixty on the globe. As always, sealed and protected against ecological poachers. We can use their video alarm system. Once we hit that and broadcast, they can't stop us. And I don't think that they will think we'll try to get there."

I looked at the map. There were several inches between Rim City and the intersection.

"Yeah," said Candy. "It's about eight hundred kilometers as the eagle flies." They wouldn't think of us tackling something like that.

After we were a kilometer into the forest we buried the blood-encrusted tolong and Candy's dress. We put on the survival overalls. Both of us had good walking shoes. We walked.

I did not talk about what had been reverberating in my mind since I glimpsed the zombies. I did not think I had seen my old body among them. But they were all big, healthy young males. It would not have been out of place. Candy must have known I was happier not talking about it.

XVI

> Learning to love others' bodies is a way of learning to love your own. She must interact with bodies. And not just with humans. Rejection is still a possibility.
>
> —I. F. + S. C. Operation Logbook

Something was following us. Some animal. Probably sampling the waddlers' carcasses we left behind. Candy had heard something two days back. And last night I had caught a glimpse of sleek grayish fur when an odd flare of the fire lit up some bushes.

And now I was caught against a rock wall. The bushes stirred. First the large light-gray eyes. They flashed red when the cat looked toward the setting sun. Toward me, that is.

Then the long, lithe gray-green body, emerging from the bush in such a manner that one thought of a hologram. It was the size of a young lion. Bigger than a leopard. And it was not a hologram. I could see the grass moving where the front claws flexed in the soil, gripping, readying. The tail, last to emerge from the bush, switched back and forth.

When you face danger, suddenly time slows down. You notice details. What struck me was how healthy, how vital, how muscular, the body was. No domestic animal I had ever seen looked so alive, so beautiful. The ears went back against the cat's skull. The canines were enormous.

I wanted to run but I knew that would just have the cat on my back.

I was weary and wary. We had been upcountry for ten days. Dodging the stingers, smacking at the biting insects, discovering waddlers as a good food source, above all trying to find a way through the scrub forest that covered most of this portion of the continent. Our way was about eight hundred kilometers as the eagle flies. A good hard walk of twenty days or so if you had a straight road. But we had no road. And we could not move on a straight like an eagle.

Like Candy, I had a number of bites on my face, neck, ears, hands, and ankles. Some were from flying insects but many and the worst were from what we called stingers. Stingers were birds, not insects. They had feathers, wings, mini-talons, and didn't taste half bad roasted, though there wasn't enough meat on them to bother with. They looked like hummingbirds in operation. Except when they dived at you. And it was nasty when they hit you.

They were on us halfway through the first morning. That was shortly after we had hit the fourth and main tributary, C-4, of the river Alph. The river Alph that ran past Rim City when it reached it some thirty-five kilometers south. Stingers turned out to be more common around any sort of water. But we had little choice about being close to water. The only effective way for a small number of people with nothing but a map to navigate through relatively thick brush or forest is by following rivers.

Aside from stinger and insect bites, we had a number of scratches and bruises from our battles with brush and undergrowth. Most of this final kind of damage came from our first blundering push to put distance between ourselves and the burning helicopter.

Pushing, tearing, and snapping branches, half tree-and-bush climbing as much as walking, we had got through about half a kilometer when Candy slowed us. We could hear the angry *chop-chop* of three or four helicopters. This was where we had changed. I stuffed my torn and bloody tolong and Candy's bedraggled dress into some sort of animal hole under a tree. We pushed some dirt on. We put on the coveralls. They had come out of two tubes in the survival kit. Made of unfashionable garlon, they had a sleazy look. Unisize adjusting, they fit reasonably well after ten minutes of moving about in them. (Garlon, spun molecule-fine and woven into a surface with superreflective aluminum, was the material for the sails that space stations used to regain the orbital height lost when they swooped to pick up packet boats. Enormously wide garlon sails and solar-light pressure to push them.)

Once or twice a helicopter had swept over us. But they had given no sign that they noticed us. We went on more quietly. Some three hours later we had made it several kilometers into the forest. I had been panting for most of it. My feet had hurt and I could feel the beginnings of blisters. My coverall had been soaked with sweat.

"Enough, let's rest. And see what we've got." Candy looked tired too. But she was obviously in much better shape than I.

We hadn't much. The medkit. Philex and some more mechanical blood-stoppers. Some broad-spec duramides, pain-killing orthoamines. A bug repellent that lasted us two days. Some experimental stinger repellent that didn't work. Two pairs of visual-radiation glasses, both soon to be broken. Some antifungal salve. Some solar-radiation protective cream. An all-purpose knife-tool.

The two overalls. Three days' food and water. A pop tent. The whole survival kit was designed to send calls for help and to keep people alive wherever their helicopter crashed. It was not intended for traveling, nor was it designed to last. We had a surprise ahead on that score.

An inflatable boat. The heaviest item was the forty-eight-hour continuous-broadcast survival beacon. The sort that is broad frequency and carries no message except the endless *beep-beep* of interplanetary distress. The second heaviest item was the visual beacon, a beta-carbon arc lamp. Both beacons would first bring people who would kill us. Neither could send a message.

We left the radio and light beacons and the inflatable boat. Heavy, useless. If we could make the Federation video station, we could get off a real message. So it wouldn't matter who got to us first. The radio beacon contained our only direction-finder. As the instructions for setting the continuous broadcast indicated, there was a compass inside—but we had no way of telling what it said. It was just for automatic broadcast. Leaving the stuff behind us was like burning a bridge.

The next few days had been composed of two realities. One reality was the map.

The large-scale tourist's map was a version of the original Federation survey map of 2110—a scaled-down version of the portion of the survey mapping that consisted of a Mercator projection square, the 3,000-by-3,000-kilometer section of Rim that had Rim City as its center. It had ditonic color branching, so you had a color scale both for height and for vegetative character.

There had not been anything significant in the way of mountain ridges on the scrub lands that could help us as a route. What we had were rivers. River C-4 was a tributary of Alph. If we could get to C-4, and be sure it was C-4, we would be able to go north along the river until we hit the Increase Mountains, better than halfway to the Federation video station. In any planet with significant vegetation, rivers and ridges are the natural paths.

We had moved what we thought was east the morning of our first day upcountry. Our goal was to meet C-4 and to follow it north. The forest then was low and matted. Trouble to push through. The brush was worse to get through, more problems about where your shins might scrape, about where your feet might hit ground.

The map had been one reality. The other was what was assaulting all our senses. What we were enduring was one of the most familiar Earth-plane forms of vegetation, something you'd find on Ceta Tau II or on Vega—or on any planet of normal formation with roughly the Earth's mass and much the same mean yearly amount of solar radiation and precipitation.

We moved slowly through low-lying, partially marshy brush-and-low-tree-covered temperate forest. Arrays of insects surrounded both of us with a buzzing nimbus. The days were warm and heavy with moisture. If you know vegetation well you might have been able to tell you weren't on Earth, or whatever. I couldn't tell the difference from the plants.

But the sky was different. The blue was somehow more blue, more intense, deeper, and at the same time the sun itself gave you less of a yellow or red light. It was warm, hot, but it somehow didn't look hot. We came to keep our skins out of the light as much as possible, and we used our protective lotion on hands and face. Rim's sun burned you quicker than Earth's Sun.

I had been dazed by the helicopter crash and the blundering slog through the undergrowth that followed. When we got out of the pop tent the next day I felt scared. I realized how significant a decision Candy had made for us. The survival beacons were some kilometers back, unrecoverable. Every step we took made it more difficult for us to turn back to Rim City. We had food for six days on half rations. We would have to find some—what?—on our way. Our hope then seemed to be to follow rivers, and eventually some mountain ridges, which would also serve to orient us on the map. And then we'd hit the automatic-tracking video station.

Before I seamed up my overalls, I got out the folding knife-tool and cut a hole. My tail hung out free from then on. No more need for concealment. I was soon to find that it helped to have a third hand for brush.

"First we get to the river. Should take us a couple of hours. We just head for where the sun is rising. The river is long enough, so we can't miss it."

Then Candy took more than half her share of going first, breaking trail. We were on our way shortly after dawn, fortified by the first of twelve survival-pack synthoprotein bars. It was to be at least noon before we hit River C-4. And the stingers were on us hours before then.

I have said that stingers look like hummingbirds. The first flight of four or five had bright-blue plumage. I was cheered by their appearance. Until one landed on my shoulder and sent its razor-sharp bill through my coverall into my back. Over the running battle that then followed, Candy got two minor stabs and I got four more wounds. But none of these compared to my first bite.

Slapping and stumbling, stumbling and slapping. Slog.

We soon were better at dodging them and scaring them off. But this slowed our progress through the brush. Eventually we found that it was best to stick to areas with some tree cover. Not thick enough to trouble our sense of direction but thick enough to cause the stingers flying problems. They were terrible pests. Even with tree cover they still got to us. The tree cover was better, though. Instead of stumble, slap, stumble, slap, it was more like stumble, stumble, stumble, slap, and so on.

Every few minutes of painful progress through the low-lying forest brush seemed like an eternity. That first morning my coverall was sodden no matter the miracles of garlon fabric. My lips had little crusts on them. I could feel the water moving around in the blister on my left foot.

We broke into a clearing and I saw the glistening, deep-blue water of C-4. I pulled off my pack and threw myself into the water. The blessed coolness enfolded me. I drank and splashed.

Candy at that point was standing on the bank, looking annoyed and wary.

"Think about this place, damn it," she said. "The river might be a good place for hunters. The ones we might hunt, you've scared. And you've advertised us to the ones who might hunt us." Well, of course I had to admit that Candy was right.

We didn't know much about the local plants and animals. The place looked like Earth. A vacation wonderland ought to have something like some of the favored plants and animals of Earth. Plus the local ecological inevitabilities, like the biting insects. But the stingers had been a surprise. I now realized that I had heard something about stingers, or something very similar. Someone had called them bee-bees (maybe from *biting birds*, or *barb-birds*, or whatever).

And Candy had heard of kill cats and groaners. The local equivalents of lions and bears.

But more important to us were what we came to call waddlers. And we had heard nothing of them in Rim City.

Candy was quiet for most of the rest of that first full day upcountry. We slogged upstream, upcountry, for the rest of the day. Each of us alone in weariness and the endless putting of one foot in front of another. We put up the tent just before sundown that day and lay down exhausted. I woke an hour or so after sunset. I felt tired and bit up. I did have that blister and some muscles were sore. But I didn't feel half bad. It's good to use your muscles.

Candy was asleep. Asleep and shivering. She had

more stinger bites than me now. Partly it was that my tail was good at fending them off. Partly it was that I had been doing much of the path-breaking as we went upriver. The path-breaker's back is protected by the person behind.

Candy was shivering as much from exhaustion as from the rapid evening cooling. I pulled the filament-foam thermal cover over most of Candy. Her face looked grayish in the fading light. I realized then that her physical resources were limited, however hard she pushed herself. She was lanky. A little over a meter and a third in height, less than forty kilos in weight. Thin. Eleven years old physically. I realized only at that point that I was stronger than she. And I realized that I could endure more physically.

It was quite dark when I really noticed the stars. The day had been cloudless. The dark was dusted with diamonds. If you have always lived on an over-populated world like Earth or even a well-populated world like Vega, you will not know the splendor of that night.

Rim, pollution- and moon-free, is an extraordinary theater for stars. I was outside now, staring at the familiar constellations. Rim was less than thirty light-years from Earth. Not enough of a distance to change many constellations. I felt at home seeing them.

Of course, while much of the celestial sphere was familiar, our angle to it was different. What must be Capella was directly overhead rather than on the horizon. And Capella was brighter than Sirius in Earth's sky. No more than five light-years away, at a guess. I saw Orion over the direction that the river took upcountry. Roughly north. Orion's sword was gone. However, the belt and the four great stars were intact, blazing in the black sky.

But then something came to me. Orion was due north on Rim. It wasn't just north now, it was the north axis of the celestial sphere. Moving us to a different angle with respect to the enduring constellations meant that the belt of Orion was roughly in the same position that Polaris, the North Star, held on Earth! I did not know how I knew this. But I knew it. Orion was north on this world. I knew this in the way that you know something from a thousand clues that you pick up unconsciously. I knew that Orion's belt, the midmost portion of that four-starred, four-limbed great hunter—I knew that Orion's belt was true north. North.

"How do you know Orion is north?" said Candy from the tent. I did not realize that I had spoken.

And then I had a sense of diagrams in my mind. Diagrams, rotating images that I had no names for. Orion just had to be in the slot to stay true north. I knew, I knew through Sally Cadmus' body, a body whose nervous system and lower brain or whatever held a sense of direction just as they held a system for directing the basic unconscious pattern of heart-muscle movements that moved the body's blood from lung to limb. "I just know it's north," I said to Candy.

We would come to use Orion as an aid to navigation. The constellation was visible before the full darkness of night. We used it to select a distant landmark. A distant, distinctively positioned mountain top, for example. Then you could use that mountain as your north for a day or two. Helped, particularly in overcast weather.

We restricted ourselves to half rations to make the food last six days. On the morning of the second day upcountry, Candy told me what we should look for for food. "We have got to find our ecological niche," said Candy rather solemnly.

"Though we're sampling the berries, they won't provide solid nourishment. And lots of things are after the berries too. Those groaner bears and a whole host of birds and small mammals.

"We can't compete with animals in what they can

do too—like run after things and grab them. Any animal *we* can catch by running or grabbing would have been wiped out long ago by predators.

"So we need a way of catching a meal that requires our special talents—intelligence, use of tools. Like something stationary with a protective shell. We have our folding knife to open the shell."

Candy went on while we were checking out the river, without much success. No clamlike creatures, unless you count snails. Something shrimplike and fast. Didn't manage to catch any fish on that or any other day.

"Another example is the porcupine. Its quills stop any ordinary mammal or reptile. Because it's so protected it waddles about, slow enough for a human to catch it, knock it out with a heavy tree limb, and then get to the meat through the unprotected belly. We need something like that."

Candy was off over the bank to a bush with the small reddish berries that we had already decided were edible.

"Though I can't say these aren't half bad." Her lips were reddish from the berries. Candy didn't have my endurance but she was resilient. Her body didn't have my heavy, musky smell, either. Two days sleeping together in the same clothes had already taught us that.

We found our porcupines on the morning of the third day upcountry. We called the first one we saw waddler. Imagine a gray turtlelike creature, half to a meter long in the shell, a little more if you counted the stubby but powerful head and limbs.

It took us about a minute to realize that we'd found our ecological niche. We trapped our first waddler with a combination of yells and branches driven into the ground. We levered it on its back so we could get to its vulnerable spots. Then we rekindled last night's fire and jock eyed the upside-down waddler carcass into the middle of the fire.

We found that the waddler's undershell would crack open if you turned the waddler right side up halfway through cooking and then upside down again at the very end. The limbs and back muscles made a good meal for two. The rest we didn't eat. I wouldn't have traded a morsel of it for more synthoprotein bars. Or for some *glenna un petit,* for that matter.

We found more waddlers as we went upriver. We supplemented them with the berries and some onion-like thick grass that was good cooked with the waddler meat.

We had found our ecological niche. What I did not realize until some days later is that the ecological niche works more than one way. We had found a way of using a portion of the environment. What we did not see is that another portion of the environment would use us.

And so we worked north, upcountry along the river that was to take us over six hundred kilometers on our journey. The river that was to be our companion for endless weeks. Though we got better at dealing with the stingers and the insects and the brush, each day was a struggle. Upcountry.

On the evening of the ninth day we looked over our bodies inside the netting of the tent. The fire gave us enough light to do the usual checking for wee crawling things, bloodsuckers, and so on.

I noticed two livid spots on Candy's shoulders.

"What are those?" I asked. They weren't recent bites. More like a freckle but flat to the skin and purplish. Candy screwed her head around to get a look at them.

"Those are the stinger bites I got on the first day. You got one like them on your neck too. Those are scars. Centuries ago people used to get them whenever they got any sort of real wound."

I had heard of scars, of course. A few people probably still have them for one reason or another. But modern medicine can stop them from happening, or remove them if you happen to acquire some outside the reach of a surgery. Scars. I expected we'd acquire more before we were through.

"Our descent into the primitive," said Candy. She lay flat out, relaxed.

And then, in the sudden light of a flare-up of the fire, I saw sleek grayish fur disappear into the brush. It happened so quickly that I wasn't sure I had really seen something. I connected it in my mind with the crashing noise Candy had heard yesterday. After listening for a while I turned to tell Candy of it but she was already asleep. I forgot to mention it the next morning.

And now, late next day, with the sun drooping down the rock wall behind me, a very large cat. Size of a young lion. The sunset lighting was what changed the cat's eyes from milky gray to reddish when it looked directly at me.

What happened for the next few minutes is in some ways still quite real to me. As if it happened in hologrammic slow motion, with stop frames, and in color more vivid than real life.

But the experience is divided in focus. Two lines of clear, narrow separate experience. One was the advance of the cat, ambling slowly forward—every detail, every change of ear position, of paw, of haunch, of eyelid, every step forward. That reel runs along through memory.

The other focus is an inner voice, myself talking to myself.

If you are to understand what these minutes were like, you have to imagine the infinitely graceful and wholly fearful movements of the cat as it came to me. And you have to listen to what that inner voice was saying, and saying as fast as possible, like a coach talking an athlete through some particularly complicated maneuver.

Imagine the cat.

Bigger than you. Probably weighs close to eighty kilos. Got to be much stronger and faster than you. A cat half its size could wipe you.

Okay, get back a bit. Behind you is the rock wall.

Watch the cat, watch it. Don't lose its eyes. Face it, you, face it. You can't run from it. Just keep looking, keep looking, baby. Hold its eyes.

Crouch, squat. On your hams. Back against the rock wall. Hand up in front. That's the way they tell you to deal with big dogs. Squat. Less of a target that way.

Now it's stopped. Okay, keep looking, keep looking. No fast movements, you, no fast movements.

You can't run, so you got to depend on fear or affection. And it's going to have to be a mix. Can't scare it. Not really.

Hold its eyes. Watch it, watch it. It's still at least five meters away. The ears are no longer folded back. It's showing you its fangs. Okay, okay, keep holding the eyes. The ears are still up. Why don't you show it your fangs?

You have got to know how to get along with this cat. Cats don't kill their own kind. Think cat. Be a cat. If it shows fangs, you show fangs. Learn to hiss.

Okay, it's only a body's length away. Crouching. Ears back. Watch it. Watch it. Tail is moving. Okay, okay, let's toss a stone over to the right. Slow hand motion, quick flip. Distract it.

Okay, now give it a little hiss. Got it off balance.

Ears are up again.

Okay, start talking to it. Slow, even, friendly tone. Talk to it.

Okay, it's coming closer. Keep looking at it and don't move a muscle. Don't move. Its ears are up and its mouth is closed. Closer, baby, baby, don't move.

And then an utterly surprising thing happened. The cat slid forward. Its head from nose to ear rubbed along my hairline from forehead to ear.

The cat moved back. Dazed, as if out of a fog, I saw the cat, upper lip screwed up, sniffing the air with a look in its eyes that an animal gets when it is concentrating on an odor, savoring an odor.

Then the cat laid itself flat. Not looking quite at me but keeping me in mind. Since it was less than five meters away, I didn't feel like trying to sneak away. I relaxed some of my iron-tight muscles and leaned back against the rock face. I regretted that I didn't have some turtle meat with me.

I had plenty of time to take in the alarming beauty of its muscles. And the sensuous grace that went into all its movements. This was the kill cat. I had not been able to decide on its sex. Recalling the name "kill cat," I also recalled that it was a hermaphrodite, coming into one sex or the other for a week or two in four-month cycles.

But the cat never the kill cat for me. At first it was the cat, later the Cat or Cat.

After letting me look at it for those few but endless minutes, the cat once more sauntered over to me. I went into my full defensive posture. The cat snarled, almost perfunctorily. I did my best to snarl. The cat then meandered off into the bush.

I waited, motionless, heart thumping, for five or ten minutes, now in full shadow from the setting sun. No more signs of the cat.

I got up to walk the hundred meters back to camp. Halfway there I heard a snapping sound behind me and dropped to the ground. I heard a swish of air and felt hot breath near me for a fraction of a second. And then I saw the cat landing less than a body's length in front of me. It looked back at me, eyes glowing. It gave something of a bark. And then it bounded off into the bush.

I had to remember that cats play with one another. Play rough. Play on the edge of being serious. Playing at preying.

Though I felt shaken, I also felt exhilarated as I returned to the campfire. I told Candy of my encounter, though I didn't mention the closeness of it.

Candy suggested that we bury or burn the extra waddler meat so that the cat would have no reason to follow us. I argued that what we had left each day was probably plenty for the animal. It wouldn't have any reason to attack us if the food supply held. There were plenty of waddlers.

Afterwards I wondered whether what I said really made sense. I knew I wanted to see the cat again. Was I intoxicated by the danger? I could hear the quizzical little bark that had been the last sound the cat had made. I saw great Orion appearing in the north, diamonds against the ever-darkening blue. Was I the hunter or the hunted?

Next day I could sense that the cat was near us once or twice. At evening I once again walked some distance from where we had camped.

This time the cat bounded at me. Three heart-wrenching bounds, a couple of meters apiece, and then it swerved to one side of me.

Down, I said to myself, and keep eyes locked. Move slow. If it's going to run by your head again, see if you can't rub its back as it goes by. Like a bullfighter with a bull, yes. You rub heads like the matador scrapes close to the bull as it goes by. Your hand in a trailing caress like the end of the matador's cape. Turn, keep your hands up, lock eyes, watch it coming in until it ducks its eyes down. Again. Pass. Again.

And sometimes you have to slow the passes down. Playing too passionately is close to letting go. Distract it. Slow matters down.

On some of the passes that second night with Cat, I could hear it. A low, rough, rumbling purr.

We continued these strange twilight trysts for days. I did not tell Candy. The long day of trekking up-country was enough to occupy us. Candy would fold up just before dusk for a nap, or for the whole night. And I would go off to meet the cat.

I played a strange sort of mental bookkeeping about what I was doing. I told myself that I could not be in real danger because the Cat had plenty to eat. And anyhow, the Cat clearly regarded these meetings as social occasions—it kept out of view during the day, kept out of Candy's vision. On the other hand, I also told myself that each of these meetings was an accident. An unplanned coincidence.

These meeting usually started with at least one repetition of the head rub-by that had been our first surprising contact. On the third evening, turning back after the rub-by, Cat leaped forward with a little bark and instantly had all four canines in my left shoulder, over the collarbone. I kept my squat, motionless. I felt Cat's hot breath. I could smell Cat's heavy smell, leathery and faintly urinous.

We were both motionless for several of Cat's pants. I realized that Cat's canines were more holding than biting. I scratched Cat along its throat and chest. I had begun my usual chatter to Cat, soothing, playful, and, I hoped, with no hint in my voice of the pain and fear I felt.

I slapped at Cat's back flank with my tail. Distraction. Then I tried being just a little stern. "Off, Cat, now off. You play too rough. Off, Cat."

And then, suddenly, Cat was licking my hair with great sweeps of its rough tongue. And again, Cat was in that pose, upper lip screwed up, sniffing away at the odors in and on its nose and tongue. This body

—its (my) odor—was all that stood between me and death.

This minor confrontation produced a further breakthrough. That third night we began to play. A restrained version of patty-cake, hand open, against paw, claws retracted. Jumping over each other. Squinching down under cover, eyes looking out just above it, mock stealthy, and the other pretending to bumble up unaware. In all of it my wild and heady wonder was that I was playing there in Rim's twilight with a creature little more than my weight but so well equipped with teeth, claws, and muscles that it could have the life from me in seconds.

My heart, my body, was complete in that twilight clearing with Cat. There was no sense of uncertainty in our motions, no sense of forethought or mistake. Innocent of compromise. When I got back near the tent I finally checked my wounds. Only one of the canines had done more than bruise the skin. That one wound looked like no more than a medium stinger bite.

On the fifth night, when I struggled down into our tent, Candy was awake.

"You know that you are absolutely crazy, don't you?" she said.

The dying fire's glow lit up her blond hair. But her face was dark.

"I followed you and watched you with your animal friend. I gather that's where you've been off to the last few nights. You're absolutely crazy." She moved her face toward me and the firelight sparkled in her eyes and across her lips. "Not unimpressive, Patty. You looked very good there. The two of you looked very good."

And now the face was very close.

"And I'll tell you something else, Patty dear. Something I don't think you may have noticed. Because if you had noticed it, you'd probably already have been demanding we recruit your damn lion.

"Have you noticed that where that creature of yours is there aren't any stingers?" Candy grinned at me, her full face now in the firelight.

"You were really impressive, my ecological nicher."

And Candy kissed me.

The next day Cat knew. It let us see it several times during the day. And late in the day, when we settled down to roast a waddler, Cat settled into the edge of the clearing, a couple of meters from me and a much more respectful distance from Candy. There were no stingers.

We made great progress the next three weeks. Mostly Cat traveled within a few meters of us. That meant no stingers.

I saw why one time when Cat had been away for the better part of an hour. A flight of two of the reddish stingers peeled off and dived on Candy. Just as the first was about to hit Candy I caught a gray-green streak in the corner of my eye. And there was Cat going by, a hair's breadth away from Candy, with both stingers down, one in Cat's teeth, the other smashed to the ground.

Cat gulped the stinger in its mouth and then ambled over to the one on the ground, picked it up, and presented it to me. I took it respectfully. Candy watched all this without moving. To that point Cat had never been closer than a couple of meters to her.

Since it was close to camp time, I set down the pack, popped the tent, and started to put a fire together. That was how I discovered the taste of stingers. You didn't think that I was so far gone as to eat the thing raw, did you? Not yet, anyhow.

I felt better at the end of the three weeks upcountry. My body was harder and tauter. The kilometers came easier. The sloughing part of the day lengthened from something like two-thirds of the daylight to three-quarters. If anything, the days were a degree or two cooler. We could tell our progress by coordinating what we saw of tributaries and lakes with our map. There was enough of geographical feature for us to be reasonably sure we had it right. Though Candy had taken to pronouncing C-4 so that it sounded like *cipher*.

XVII

A successful implant displays acceptance at the deepest and most primitive levels of being. Where self and the other become one.

—I. F. + S. C. Operation Logbook,
Append. III, The Chief's Report

Candy leaned against the mouth of our cave. We had fixed the side of her coverall with philex but it was frayed and loosening again. The garlon of our coveralls still kept us fairly warm but it was going. From the time unicouple material leaves the tube it has a limited life in the air. All coverall seams up, Candy was not quite shivering.

"You know even Cat didn't try to go out this morning. Yesterday it had trouble right away. Practically buried itself in the dip just below the cave mouth. And then just struggled back."

Candy didn't have to say that we were in trouble. We were a good portion through the Increase Mountains when the snow began to fall, gently, softly. That was evening three days ago. By next morning the snow was a quarter of a meter to a meter deep. The day was bleak and dim, foggy when it wasn't snowing. We couldn't see our landmarks—particularly the twin peaks, on the map KP and KB, that we needed to keep just to our west as we passed by. And we couldn't see our footing. Stumbling, sliding, falling, we gave up after less than a hundred meters. We felt lucky to make it back to the cave.

The next day was even bleaker and dimmer and the snow fell more thickly, silently. Only Cat tried a walk. And lay panting, wet and steamy, after nearing losing itself. What had I brought Cat to? I didn't think it could get out of here any more than we.

The last of our carefully dried and lightly toasted waddler meat now smelled sweetish. Just a touch of putridity. It was nearly gone in any case. The two-liter container that I had stocked with turtle fat for the Cat was drained. Nothing left but the rancid smell. The cave was full of heavy, dubious odors. We had expected to be through the pass of the Increase Mountains by yesterday at the latest. We had less than a day's rations left. Scraps. And the cold burned off our calories even if we weren't walking.

There was no wood for burning, no fire. Water we had by letting snow warm in a poly bag. That cost our heat inside the cave. And Candy was using plenty of water by then. Fever.

Before, we had slept Candy next to me and the Cat on the other side—when it chose to lie there, as it did more frequently as we ascended.

That night I eased Candy over next to Cat after she had fallen fully asleep. Between us she had as much warmth as she could get. I laid awake while Cat and Candy slept. Awake, Candy was nervous about Cat. Both asleep, they moved easily against each other, shifting position in harmony. Cat's odor was heavy in the air. I felt good about that.

What was I to do with them?

Later Candy awoke, fever down for a bit. She whispered to me while Cat slept.

"There's a poem by a twentieth-century poet. Dylan Thomas." Candy's voice was husky, congested. The skin of her face was taut over the cheekbones and eye sockets, and the skin was reddish from the weather and her fever.

"The first nympher I ever knew read it to me. And

when I took up harmonizing too, I read it to my first student, a guy who'd trained as a vampire. A trained psychetician but he wanted to get into the real center of mind implant—the place where you form a way of living from the mind tapes and the body's latencies. Harmonizing memories and reflexes. Sensory ins. Motor outs.

"The poem's about the way in which what makes up your body goes back into living things when you die. Part of you may become muscle tissue in a squirrel or a segment of the husk of an ear of corn. A bit of your amino acid may end up as a flexor in a neurological lattice of some late-twenty-second-century human."

Candy's voice was distant, automatic, slow. The winds that had followed the last deadly snowfall were still. In the breaks between Candy's words I sometimes heard the faint whistle of Cat's breathing.

"I am eighty years old. I am cynical enough, weary enough, scattered enough, aching enough, to say that."

I stroked Candy's forehead. My cool, trail-roughened fingers against that heat.

"I tell myself that I am eighty. But what is eighty?

"This body that I am, that is dying in this snow-locked trap, is eleven years old. It is so lithe and agile, so young, so bloody costly . . ."

Her hand closed over mine.

"You know I haven't—it hasn't—had a period yet. I felt a tremor of a cramp on *Pequod* and an itch in my nipples. Now I will end without it."

I knew that Candy had had her last implant. Her mind was past the limit for implant. By law no tapes would have been made for her. She would die altogether.

"I have sent five bodies into the world," the slow, monotonous voice continued. "I even saw the first one die a few years back. The body was sixty-odd and not too viable—too old for the ghouls to use. And the mind was right up against ninety-five plus.

"You know"—Candy gave a slight humorless chuckle—"you know I was her designated next of kin? I had to see her through it. Not pleasant.

"I got so stung by it that I began to think about illegal rejuvenation. It's something the vampires don't talk about. They stop doing transplants after mental-age eighty because they have a high failure rate. They also stop because even if you seem to make implant and overcome rejection, you get a body-shredding reaction.

"If you succeed in implanting a ninety-year-old mind, the body you set it in starts to age and break down like crazy. They did it a couple of times back in the 2050's when implanting got started. Fact is, Bruhler's equations predict that a ninety-year-old mind will chew up an implant body at ten times the normal rate. And at ninety-five, it will be close to fifty times.

"That means that if I had been able to implant her ninety-six-year-old mind successfully, she would age a nympher body into physical old age within a year. The next one would take maybe a quarter of a year. And so on. You'd run through a whole supply of young bodies. Funny how you think of things like that."

There was a long pause, punctuated by a snort from Cat that momentarily interrupted its slow breathing.

"So she, my first nympher body, died. And I will die here, it seems. But not the other bodies I brought up.

"Suppose that there was a tape of me left somewhere. Suppose they'd played it in on a body and it worked. Would that mean that I was still alive? There's no direct line between this body and that consciousness, between what I now am and that medical event. What if someone were just born who happened to develop a mind a lot like mine? That person might be more like me now than a real implant. So how can it make sense to say that the implant is more me than the mind that is more like me?

"I remember my third body. What a personality I had then. I was a whole lot different from what I was in my fourth and fifth bodies. You are *both* your Bruhler-equation mental structure *and* the physical brain and body that are shaped by and that shape those structures."

Candy's fingers closed hard on mine. I felt her eyes on me.

"Who are you, Patty?

"The body of Sally Cadmus has been interacting with what was salvaged from Ismael Forth's mental life. Ismael Forth isn't left intact, or you'd be dead and the operation an implant-rejection failure. In a way Ismael Forth and Sally Cadmus are dead. In a way they are not. In a way a fifty-year-old person may contain a ten-year-old person that he was, and in a way he does not.

"The Dylan Thomas poem is titled 'A Refusal to Mourn the Death by Burning of a Child in London.' The last line of the poem is 'After the first death there is no other.'

"We're always being born and dying, my friend. When we go, how will you count the numbers?"

Candy said that last word *numbers* several times, each mouthing more indistinct than that before it. After a time her fingers loosened. Her breathing slowed into a harmony with Cat's.

I love you, Candy, but what is it that I love? That graceful and beautiful and vigorous body? That?

But it is just too easy to say that I love that agile, firm, ancient mind—that motherly mind. *Motherly*, of course, not in some patronizing and sentimental sense. Mothering.

No, I cannot say it is the mind alone that I love.

Think of her hands.

I do not know who I am. Perhaps it does not matter to us.

I could see Orion in the cave's mouth. The bright hunter was fading as I watched it. Clouds. More snow. And even a rise in temperature could not melt the snow fast enough to save us.

I awoke near dawn. The cave was a touch warmer, the air sodden with moisture. I had been awakened by Cat, who was at the cave's mouth. Cat had given a little bark. I could see Cat move forward, nose first, and then jerk back. Cat's sleek gray-green fur glistened against the mist that was whitening in the milky dawn. And then I heard something more than our breathing.

Rain. Steady, heavy beat. Warm air from the south. Water, water, endless water. Water that would clear a way through deep snow. I had not thought of rain.

Cat barked. And began licking up one of the steady trickles of water that were cutting through the snow cover above the cave's mouth. I stroked its back.

That afternoon the sun broke through the rain clouds, blue and dazzling. We were on our way. We camped well into the tree line of the northern edge of the Increase Mountains. Candy's fever was gone. We had won through. A day or two would see us on the flats. Waddlers. Food. And a week would bring us to the Federation video station.

XVIII

> When the implant starts taking over the controls, that's when you really know you're on your way.
>
> —I. F. + S. C. Operation Logbook, Append. I, Dossiers.

We soon had reason to be glad the rain had not eliminated all of the snow.

The next afternoon Cat, who was off some distance from the trail we were making, began barking. As we neared we could also hear an occasional snarl. Cat had trapped a large creature, a sort of boar, in a snow-lined gully. As we came up, the boar was swinging its murderous-looking tusks from side to side, snorting at Cat. The boar's legs barely kept its stomach above the snow. It could not move quickly. Cat stood surefooted at the snowless edge of the gully, snarling when the furious boar tried to move out of the snow.

The boar looked near Cat's weight and its tusks looked like they could do nasty work. Cat was hungry. (We were hungry.) But evolution makes a carnivore cautious about attacking a creature its own size, particularly one with good defensive weapons. Cat would stand a fair chance of getting badly hurt by those tusks. No carnivore can afford such risks as a steady diet. Solitary lions and wolves live mostly on mice and other small rodents. And the snow which was hampering the boar's movements would give Cat trouble too.

We were far enough below the tree line so that here

and there straight-branched hardwoods were replacing the scraggly, gnarled softwoods that fringed the stony upper slopes. Candy was cutting away at the branches with the knife-tool. While we hurried at making two spears, I was much more aware of the need to help Cat before it made a serious attack on the boar than I was of any need for food. Danger is a marvelous eliminator of hunger.

It was a clumsy business. One I'm not too happy thinking about. Suffice it to say that after many attempts Candy and I pinned the boar momentarily and Cat took lethal hold of the back of the boar's neck. The savage grace of Cat's final attack compensated for the shameful clumsiness of the badgering thrusts Candy and I had contributed.

Within a few minutes Cat, full-bellied, was methodically and contentedly licking its claws. Candy and I were not to stuff ourselves as quickly. We set a fire but it began to rain. It was some time before we found a cave and enough dry wood to do a respectable cooking job. When we were finishing our meal, Cat woke briefly and looked out at me from the middle of the cave. Its eyes glowed with the reflected light of the fire. Cat purred. Cat stretched, still purring, and curled up next to Candy.

Certainly there was a pattern in Cat's genes. It was programmed by nature to love companions of what it loved. The hunting pack is built on such principles. So Cat loved and respected Candy because she had hunted with Cat and because Cat loved me. Candy was comfortable with Cat lying against her back. Was Candy's emotion so different from Cat's? Were thoughts so far from genes, minds from bodies? We had hunted together.

That cave was a trap for us.

Late that night we met our first groaner. A groaner

looks much like a kodiak brown bear with just a suggestion of a gorilla in its forelimbs and posture. They run up to over half a ton in weight. The one that came for us that night—crazy with some sort of determination beyond hunger—must have weighed at least three hundred kilos. Afterwards we literally could not move it out of the mouth of the cave.

For me it began all at once. I awoke hearing a crescendo of the deep, throaty, menacing pants that gave the groaner its name. At the same time I felt Cat slide by me, infinitely taut and graceful.

Candy and I grabbed for what we had used to worry the boar. Candy was closest to the cave's wide mouth. Her spear—a slightly crooked pole with a sharpened end—touched the groaner as it entered. The groaner flung Candy's pole aside like a match stick, throwing Candy against the side of the cave.

Perhaps I helped Cat by thrusting my own spear forward, perhaps not. Examining the groaner later I could see that the sharp end had failed to make it between the bear's ribs. It slid upward, slashing the bear's hide, making a superficial scratch. It was male. Its claws were like railroad spikes.

Cat, who had hesitated so long over the boar, barking and snarling, feinting and wary, now just hurtled forward, a stream of grayish fur. Cat had him around the neck. The groaner shook Cat again, and again and again, tearing at Cat's belly with long, cruel strokes of his foreclaws. And then, convulsively, Cat was thrown across the cave.

The groaner turned to me, eyes bright, almost reddish in the half light. The bear would make short work of Candy and me.

But then I saw the bright red of arterial blood on the bear's throat. Where Cat had clung for so long, with desperate determination, gouging and grinding with its jaws. The blood was pulsing rhythmically, matting the groaner's chest, throwing gouts of blood against the cave wall.

The groaner's eyes glazed. The groaner slumped. He gave a half moan, half sigh, dying.

Candy was standing next to me. Her garlon overalls were ripped from shoulder to haunch along the left side of her back. Her shoulder had some scratches where she must have hit rock when the groaner threw her. The skin was ruddy and livid. She would have a nasty bruise there tomorrow. The groaner sagged further, spreading to cover the whole lower half of the cave's mouth. There was a whispery rattling sound, and we no longer heard the groaner's heavy pants.

Cat was sprawled motionless where it had been flung. Like a garbage sack that had missed the disposal chute. When I came over, Cat moved only its eyelids, looking up at me, then letting the lids droop once more. There was blood, presumably groaner's, slopped over its muzzle. There was no heavy flow from its many belly cuts. But the groaner had done its work. There was one long wound, from rib through belly, opening the body cavity with crude surgery. I could see Cat's stomach and a bit of the tangle of its intestines.

I squatted for several minutes over Cat.

Candy took my hand, gently trying to lead me away. "It's terrible," she said. "I can't tell you how I feel about Cat. Let's get outside."

I said nothing. I did not move. Candy pulled again. "Look, we're okay. I'm a little bruised. You're shook up. But we can make it to the station. We made it this far."

I did not move. My face was wet and I was shivering.

"Come on, Patty. Come on. Cat was a marvelous friend, but it can't heal a half-meter slice like that. And any wild animal will die of infection with the body cavity open like that."

Candy pulled at me again. "Let's leave it some privacy. Come on. We got things to do."

I pushed Candy aside.

The garlon material of our coveralls had been out of the tubes for several weeks. It was beginning to fray and disintegrate. No reliable thread there. I found what I wanted in the stitching on one of the packs. Cutting freely with the knife-tool, I extracted a few lengths of thread strong enough so that I could not snap them.

The all-purpose knife-tool was the next to go. It had an awl on it the size of a large needle. Using a rock, I smashed at the middle of the tool until the pins holding the blades and other tools sheared out. I pulled the awl blade out of the wreckage of the tool. I put some of my thread through the hole that had anchored the awl to the tool. Then I savaged the medkit.

I sprinkled the entire supply of antibacterial powder into and on the lips of Cat's body cavity. As I forced my crude needle through Cat's flesh I felt an occasional jerk from Cat. It once tried to turn to look at me but failed. I tried to make reassuring noises. My hands were slippery with Cat's blood.

Afterwards, and clumsily, I hacked away at the groaner's belly with the long, now handleless, blade of the smashed tool. Cat took a few slivers of liver dosed with orthoamine sulphate from my hands before settling into a long, deathlike sleep.

I sat next to it through much of the rest of the day. Candy got me to eat a little of the leftover boar meat. The meat whose smell trail must have brought the cold-hungered groaner. I felt nauseated. After a time Candy managed to get me to lie down. I could hear Cat's shallow breathing.

Candy and I had said nothing from the time I began pulling thread out of the pack. My hands were covered with blood and my face must have been besmeared with it, for I remember wiping tears and sweat away from my eyes. Candy must have thought I was crazy. Maybe I was.

But Cat lived.

After the waiting, the rest was not difficult. Though by the time we reached the automatic-tracking Federation station three weeks later, Candy and I looked like we belonged to the stone age. The garlon overalls gave out completely, shredding and tufting and tearing like tissue paper. For two days, once we had started, we wore folds of groaner hide but they stank and attracted insects, so we set them aside. After a day it felt perfectly natural to walk naked. Out of the mountains the daytime temperatures were warm enough. We kept one pack but even that was lifted by some creature. We were still carrying stakes, mine tipped by the long knife blade, Candy's by a groaner claw. Cat was with us, almost wholly healed, breathing vitality. We got Cat moving a week after the groaner attack, though earlier we'd had to stretcher Cat out of the cave with two poles wound round with the tent. The groaner had begun to reek after two days, attracting every sort of creature.

We found the station easily enough. Fortunately it was located down in the V formed by the join of two northward-flowing rivers. At three or four kilometers distance we saw the beacon pole from a hillock near the river we were following.

Cat entered the small two-room station with us. Apart from the beacon pole and the entrance stairs, the station was below ground. Minimum ecological interference.

I do not think that I have ever felt as happy as I felt striding those last meters toward the station. I felt healthy and taut. Fifteen minutes in the station's tiny fresher took care of much of our stone-age quality. There were clothes to put on too. Simple overalls but the material felt more natural than garlon. We had called Rim City's Federation office as soon as we got inside. Though the place was called a video station, voice transmission was all that was possible. I told the increasingly excited man who answered on the emergency Federation band who and where we were. Then Candy took over to explain why we'd split. She asked for a tight beam check. Then she identified herself and explained about me and the Philpritz Modulated zombies and all. The guy picked up on it after a while and got the officer in charge on a hook. The heaver and packet personnel were nominally Federation and probably could be depended on in a showdown. We were told to get off the air unless we had a real emergency. And we were told to wait by the radio. They would be here in four or five hours by helicopter.

After freshing, the three of us half dozed. We would hear the sound of the rotors. They would be surprised by Cat. We would have to get them all inside the helicopter while we said goodbye to Cat. No point in taking risks.

In fact they came in less than three hours. And we did not hear the sound of rotors. They came by light plane, gliding the last few kilometers with silent engines, landing a few hundred meters away in a meadow. And they were not Federation.

The diethyl nitrous oxide that they fed the ventilation system flipped me from half sleep into unconsciousness. The first and last impression I had that something was wrong was just that I knew I was going to sleep too fast. Sleep did not come at you like a floor to which you were falling. Sleep did not crush you out.

XIX

> The implant mind must give up and overcome the most intimate bodily relationship that humans ever know.
>
> —I. F. + S. C. Operation Logbook, Append. III, The Chief's Report

I was shaken out of unconsciousness hand- and ankle-cuffed, with a fragmenting headache and someone on top of me. Pain was what got me half awake. My tail was mostly running down one of my legs under the coverall. But a few inches of it were uncomfortably coiled up under my buttocks and I was being pushed painfully back on it. I was still so groggy from the gas that I wasn't fully conscious. It was like a painful dream.

The person on top of me was breathing hoarsely next to my ear. Perhaps I made some sound, for the breathing paused for a moment. The person's hands were on my back. I was being hugged, rhythmically. Why?

You have to remember I really wasn't yet capable of full consciousness.

Then I realized that my coverall was unzipped down the front. And the person was male. And I felt, besides the pain in my tail and the pressure between my legs, a tingling realization. I was weightless. I was in space.

That was why the guy was hugging me. Rape is more difficult in weightlessness. A man has to pull himself into you. He can't just lift himself up and let gravity push him into you.

I suppose I was lucky that I was so groggy. On what seemed to be an emergency surgery shelf, my body was pulled flat and firmly secured by plastic cuffs. I couldn't have resisted if I had been wide-awake. Though I knew his penis had entered me, I felt more nausea than pain. When I was fully conscious several minutes later, I was to feel real soreness. As it was, I don't think he realized I was partially awake.

It went on and on. I felt humiliation and anger, yes. But abstractly, distantly. The sound of his panting and the half-articulate mumbles that began as he nearly climaxed—this hit me much more than the peculiarly distant rubbing of unprepared flesh.

Finally it was over.

I had blinked my eyes open enough to confirm that I was in a small private-business planetary ship. In particular I was in the kitchen, which normally doubles as a surgery. The light hurt. I kept my eyes closed as he got off me. What had happened?

"Pleasure before business, my little zombie maiden," he said. "Though I suppose you missed the pleasure. There'll be plenty more when you're awake. We'll have you around in a bit."

There was an evil yet familiar tone to his soliloquy. As if I were hearing a familiar voice distorted by some form of frequency modulation.

I felt the prick of a hypodermic needle. I felt a rush of warmth in my blood. My nausea washed away as I became fully awake.

"The modern methods didn't work so well with your little brat. And I had to ditch Dr. Sperling. We shall see what traditional methods will do for us.

"Wake, my dear."

That last request was coupled with a stinging slap. My eyes popped open. Wide.

Before me stood Ismael Forth. The old body.

It looked different. Nastier. Unhealthy perhaps. There seemed to be more tremor in the hand movements.

I saw, of course, the Ismael Forth *body*. I could not —cannot—say how much of the difference I saw was really there or a product of my altered viewpoint. (You have never looked directly at your own face. You have seen your face only in mirrors—or in photographs, videos, holograms. Who knows how strange your face would look to you if you could see it directly?)

At first sight I felt amazement. This lasted but an instant. It was hate at second sight. I knew who this was. This person had kidnapped Ismael Forth. And caused my first death. Those zombies Candy and I saw from the helicopter were for this maniac.

The person who had slapped me flipped around, floating, as his whirling slowed, toward what would have been the ship's ceiling under gravity. When you hit downward in weightlessness, you go upward. He obviously hadn't had a lot of experience with weightlessness. Indeed, he got his hands out just in time to save himself a good smash on the head. (One of the confusing and dangerous features of weightlessness for the inexperienced is that weight *but not inertia* is lost. If you hurtle yourself across a big room in weightlessness, you won't fall to the floor, but you will hit the wall on the other side of the room as hard as if you hurtled yourself right at the wall on Earth. They wouldn't let the passengers on *Pequod* into the weightless section because of the danger of concussion.)

Gingerly, lubberhold to lubberhold, the Ismael Forth body returned to me. Heavy, muscular, a little fat. The man who pulled himself into me was strong.

He came toward me with a collar in his hand. His lubber's slippers were once more adhering to the deck fabric. He must have slapped me quite hard to have pulled even one slipper from the deck. Now I saw that there was a metal device bonded to the back of the collar. Suddenly he had it around my neck. I jerked convulsively in all the small ways that my bonds allowed. The inner surface of the collar felt oily, used. I could smell the stale odor of an earlier occupant. I could smell vomit.

"Awake now, aren't you?" that hateful haunting voice said. "And you know what I just put on you. Your little protégée was wired up to stop Dr. Sperling's drugs. The doctor said that no one but a CID special would have that sort of psychological prep. To be sure, the doctor might have exaggerated to excuse his mistake. But you are no innocent tourist, obviously."

He looked appraisingly into my eyes. "You would do well not to make a mistake with me."

I had a Philpritz Modulator around my neck. I could feel odd twinges from my spine where the metal unit now rested.

"The doctor is now dead. He would have found it difficult to explain the implant equipment and the zombies whenever your backup team arrived. In any case I would not have him along. He's a traceable identity. I am not. I must disappear now. We have another operation."

Except for an occasional savage gleam, he had all the air of a genial doctor explaining health to an adolescent. The occasional body tremor was probably what Candy would have called a symptom of over-age implant. This person must run through bodies every few months, always on the edge of rejection and mental breakdown.

Candy, where are you?

"Now, you must understand some very simple facts. I know you are CID, a Federation agent. You have assumed the name Patricia Cabot Forth. I would have expected a fake name even if you weren't so stupidly cocky as to have taken the name of one of the zombies. I can just imagine you hotshots inventing code names like Operation Forth Filled or Forth Right. You pitiful youngsters."

He looked down at me and patted the Philpritz Modulator. "I am not a fool. Without Dr. Sperling I cannot do a full synch integration. I cannot order you about through this P.M.

"But that probably doesn't matter. Anyone wired up to stop interrogation drugs would probably explode if you tried genuine Philpritz control. Sperling said that and I am sure he was right. He also said it would be perfectly safe to use the P.M. as I'm using it. Just as a device to paralyze your voluntary muscles.

"Pity if he's wrong and you die before I'm finished. But I need the control over you. Particularly since some of what I intend for you may mean I'll have to take off your cuffs. Of course I am much stronger than you but there's very little point in being incautious.

"You'll also find that the kinds of paralysis I can produce with the P.M. are very convincing, very—how am I to put it?—painful. Just fiddling with the P.M. There were two bodies that turned out to have hidden discontinuities. Couldn't take me as implant. So I played with them to find out what you could do with just a nonsynched P.M. You will find that your most fervent wish is that your father and mother never met. You'll pray for death like a thirsty man for water.

"But I have more powerful means than P.M. More powerful. More traditional, certainly, and more bloody. Medieval in the original sense.

"That's a time I've always felt I was from. I should have been a medieval prince. Or perhaps a fanatic Puritan, as my name suggests. And we are now at the first stage of that subtle sequence that they understood so well then. I am showing you the instruments, Pat dear."

He turned a switch that put me and the operating shelf upright with respect to the room.

"There, there, now," he said, zipping up my coverall partway. "Think of me as your doctor."

He pulled a control chip from his pocket and puched a few keys.

I felt the horribly desperate feeling you get when you are drowning, when you can't get any air into your lungs. And I couldn't move a muscle, though every part of me was screaming *Move, move anywhere, move anything, MOVE.*

Then it stopped and I could see him again. He waved the control chip in front of me.

"First instrument. A very mild demonstration."

He patted my cheek.

"My dear Patricia Forth, permit me to introduce myself. I am Norman Saylor Mather. My mind is ninety-seven years old and nothing, absolutely nothing, is going to stop me living out the years I can add by frequent implantation. Nothing.

"As an experienced special you must have understood—even before I mentioned my name—that I cannot let you live. But you are going to find out that there are many worse things than death, my dear. There is only one question between us: that is whether or not you are going to die in the comparatively painless way that your partner Candy did when Dr. Sperling's drugs tripped her special self-destruct circuits."

Candy, I will kill him for you somehow. I swear it, Candy.

"Oh, you didn't know she was dead, did you? Oh, yes." He smiled again, the genial doctor. "Yes. You know, we started on her first just because you got an extra dose of the gas. You rolled over next to one of the vents.

"So we flew you straight back to the manor underground. Had to leave a man behind to get you back.

"Sperling said you weren't going to be out of it for

hours, even with a little help. But we got the kid out real quick. Then Sperling gave her something to open her up and she turned cyanotic the moment the drug hit her vein.

"Hated to see it happen. It would have been amusing to have played around with her. Attractive.

"Then we knew we were in trouble. You weren't innocent tourists who stumbled on something. Stumbled on something that even an innocent would realize was so illegal that the baddies would want them dead. You were agents and there was someone behind you. So we had to get out of there. And we'd take you because we still neeeded to find out what you knew.

"I didn't *want* to kill Sperling. But he couldn't come and he could be interrogated. Besides, he had blundered."

He spoke as if he *wanted* to convince me that he had been rational rather than merely angry, crazy angry. I will kill him for you, Candy.

"So I got out of there fast. Me and my baggage —you and few instruments—took the packet. And I transferred from the station to this IBO operations yacht.

"And I am now going to find out what you know. If you cooperate I promise you a painless death. Yes?"

He paused. I said a word.

"Cat?"

"Yes, the kill cat. That was quite a surprise for us. The gas didn't have as much of an effect on the animal. It could work its jaws but not its limbs. Fell over when it tried to get Mannings. I zapped it out of pure hunting reflexes. Magnificent beast. I regret I wasn't able to bring it back as a trophy. What on earth was that damned beast doing there?"

I will kill him for you.

My face must have shown him something.

"Well, my dear Pat, it isn't important for me to know that."

"There is one thing you have to understand about what happens now." He brought out what looked like a medkit bag. He talked as he opened and unpacked it.

"I am going to introduce you to torture. Something ancient that I understand quite as well as Dr. Sperling ever understood his drugs. Torture, rather than drugs, is what the ancients used to extract information. What you have to understand is the relationship between the tortured and the torturer."

He was laying out devices—modern, handmade, not manufactured devices—on a magnetized panel. His hand flicked out to give me another stinging slap. It was as hard as before but he had braced himself better so he did not lose floor contact.

"Pay attention, my dear.

"As a creature of the present age you may not have even heard of physical torture, of the efficient use of pain. You probably don't know what intense, stabbing, repeated, unending pain is. What you might think is that the torturer—that's me—applies pain until the tortured—that's you—is willing to say something. Rationally, at some point the pain will be enough to make you open your mouth.

"But it's not that simple."

He punctured this last comment with a cruel punch just below my ribs, a punch that opened my mouth.

"The problem is that the torturer has to be sure that what he is told is the truth. He has to be sure that he isn't being told lies. Most of the time the torturer can't check whether he is being told the truth.

"Suppose you tell me I will be safe down on Rim for at least another week. If I check this by waiting, and you are lying, I'm caught. So the torturer can't just force you say anything. The torturer has to own you, has to drive you so crazy with pain and fear that you'll blurt out the truth and he'll know it's the truth."

His hand snaked out and patted my cheek.

"Pain will break you, my dear. I will break you. I will be your psychotherapist, your confessor, your father, your high priest.

"You will come to fear me above all things, you will beg me for death, you will watch me like the most devout worshiper watches his god. Eventually, you will hate yourself so much that you will love telling the truth."

He reached for one of his devices.

"That's why the ancient religious torturers, the inquisitors, were the best at torture. They understood that torture is an extreme form of religious conversion.

"At some point I will know that you are so far gone in hysteria and self-contempt that I can believe what you say.

"I regret that this will mean that I will have to destroy your personality and do considerable damage to your body."

I had to remember that he wanted me to believe he was crazy. He couldn't expect me to believe his simpering and insincere regrets. But of course he was crazy anyhow, underneath his slyness. And he wanted me balled up in this paradox.

He watched me. There was a glistening of sweat on that so-familiar, so-strange face. He loves this.

He's done this before.

"I used to wonder why the medieval torturers did so much sheer damage to the bodies they worked on. If you could cause as much pain working on the surface—which is where most of the nerves are—why bother crushing a knee or an elbow? The amateurs of the twentieth century often prided themselves on not leaving even superficial marks, let alone pulverized joints. They failed to really understand the underlying psychology of torture, of body image.

"My rule is that the more gross the body damage, the less the person has to hold on to. The less—"

He slapped me again.

"Pay attention. I said the less the person has left, the easier it becomes to give up."

He held up a peculiar and crudely made pair of pliers. "This pulls out fingernails. You have no idea how painful I can make it feel.

"But this, this is my special pride."

He held up something of metal and wood that looked like a hip boot. The metal looked preindustrial, handworked. He showed me the heavy screws that contracted or expanded the boot. There was even a hammer to help the mechanical advantage of the screws.

"I bought this from the Papal Archival Museum collection. An amazing find. It was almost certainly used by Sprenger's people in the 1450's and 60's. Sprenger wrote *Malleus Maleficarum,* "The Hammer against Witches." The basic text on torture by someone who did it professionally. He showed you how you could get miserable, frightened women to confess to horrendous and wholly imaginary crimes, knowing that this confession would mean the final agony of slowly burning on the stake. He got them to *believe* they did the imaginary crimes they confessed. He got their broken, pain-seared bodies to kiss his hands in penance for the imaginary crimes. He triumphed over bodies!

"Do you know what a leg screw is, dear Pat?" he said, waving that ancient horror in my face. There were discolorations in the ancient wood. Stains. Old and new.

A centimeter of muscle spasmed rhythmically in his cheek. He put the boot aside.

"You understand that I am showing you the instruments. When the Pope let the inquisitors have Galileo, he told them they could do nothing more than show

Galileo the instruments. And they did it. Galileo recanted his own science, his pride, his life's work. All that, and all they did was talk to him. And show him how some physical instruments worked. A purely psychological victory!"

I will kill him.

He went on with his lecture for a time. There were several more devices. I did not listen much. I watched his sweating, spasming face. Grossly, he was that familiar yet strange late-twenties strong male body. Yet the little signs of tremor were appropriate to someone very old—or someone with a degenerative nervous disease. Candy had said that someone like this would chew up young bodies. How much longer could he last?

Now he was heating the tips of pencil-sized metal rods. They developed a ruddy glow inside the familiar spherical flame that weightlessness produces.

He took the Philpritz Modulator control chip from his shirt pocket. He tapped it while I tried to prepare for the suffocating horror that had happened before. But all I felt was a kind of slackness through my body. A muscular numbness. No shortness of breath.

"You will note, my dear, that you cannot move your arms or legs. With this setting you can breath and move your facial muscles and so on. But you can't move your arms and legs. You are functionally incapacitated. Helpless. You have no idea how this helplessness intensifies pain.

"But you will."

He flicked the control chip and my limbs came to life again. He came toward me with the chip in his left hand and two glowing rods in his right.

"You will notice that the human forearm is not very sensitive."

He touched the tip of one rod against my left arm. My body convulsed and I choked back a scream as the bolt of pain stabbed through me. I felt a sudden light sweat over my body. And I smelt burned flesh.

I will kill him for you, Candy. For you, Cat.

For you, Sally.

"A bit painful, yes. But notice now . . ." He flicked the control chip and my arms and legs went slack again. Then the other rod came down an inch from the first.

Horrible, intolerable, releaseless, unending pain. I heard a scream at some impossible distance from that pain that consumed me. *Etaoin shrdlu.* I felt that the crotch of my coveralls was wet and thought with mad irrelevance that in weightlessness the liquid was as likely to seep up my body as down my legs. From a distance I heard his voice.

"You see how different it is. How painful when your body is helpless. And that was an insensitive part of your skin. You'll appreciate the difference when I burn something genuinely sensitive."

He unzipped my coverall down the front and pulled it aside so that my nipples were exposed.

The video com was beeping from the control room.

Visibly, he took control of himself. He mopped his face with a handkerchief.

"That will be the manor, I expect. I will have to leave you for a bit." He checked my cuffs briefly. After glancing at the setting he put the control chip next to his other instruments. My legs and arms were still paralyzed.

"Ta, ta," he said, leaving the kitchen compartment.

I will kill.

As he left the compartment I realized that I could move my tail. It was convenient that he had unzipped the coverall. The tip of my tail is like a long multi-articulate finger coupled with a stubby thumb. In seconds I got my tail up between my legs and had the finger grasping the tongue of the P.M. collar. I could smell urine and sperm. With the collar off I went for the handcuffs. And then the hands did the legs. Free and weightless.

I dived for the compartment hatch.

There he was, over the video com, looking away from me. His head was leaned against the space-hardened glass of the midship portal.

Sometimes you do something as if you know exactly how to do it—and you do know exactly how to do it—but you have no conscious sense that you know how.

I slid myself into position against the firm hatch stanchion and pushed off like an acrobat—maximum muscle power and maximum control. I (we?) flipped half across the compartment and I came into him boots first, legs ramrod stiff, the whole inertia of my body hitting the back of his head like a hammer. Caught between my boots and the portal, his head crumpled with a dull liquid sound like a watermelon.

I think that I will call myself Sally. Sally Forth.

I spaced the body.

The video com was bust. His legs had jerked across as he died, wrecking the Vernier settings. Could be fixed but I won't bother. I could reach the Rim station by dead reckoning. I wouldn't need the radar or the computer. I suddenly realized that I probably could use the navigational computer.

Ismael Forth had never spaced. But Sally Cadmus had.

As I sat the manual controls I realized that my boots were slippery. I looked down. Mather's blood was smeared over the smooth leather of my boots. I did not think that I would clean them now.

Cat was dead. Candy was dead. And I would mourn for them later.

In the midst of death I was alive. I was myself.

Again.

XX

> Germaine Means announced that the patient is beyond rejection.
>
> —I. F. + S. C. Operation Logbook

Gxxhdt.

Etaoin shrdlu. Mmm.

Anti-M.

Away mooncow Taddy-fair fine. Fine again, take. Away, along, alas, alung the orbit-run, from swerve of space to wormhole wiggle, brings us. Start now. Wake.

So hear I am now coming out of nothing like Eros out of Death, knowing, Anti-M.

"Auntie Em," I blurted, goggling at Germaine Means. I was in a hospital bed.

"Antagonistic-Null Tracking Measure, actually," replied Germaine. "When you reach ANTM that means we have a successful implant. It seems very quick when it happens—like the point where the room flips right side up when you are wearing prism lenses that turn your image upside down. Imagine those flips happening all over the place. You're all together, mind and body." She reached and held my hand. Firmly. Flesh on flesh.

"Though I would think that Mother Em would be more appropriate than Auntie," added Germaine. Her lips quivered for a mini-second and a huge smile burst across her face. She laughed. Laughed like all the world was friends.

They—meaning François Vase, who played Mather and Brainbridge; Candy Darling, who played herself, the Other; Austin Worms, M. Herbert and so on; Germaine, who I now saw had in her a little of Trudy Double and a little of myself—they, the people who had played the characters, looked down at me.

"I trust you enjoyed your time in *Pequod,*" said Austin Worms in a right fair imitation of Chief Steward Inger. He grinned, his face flushed. "This time they let a somatician play a couple of roles too. So glad you made it."

And there was Candy, holding my eyes, half apologetic, half proud and happy. Candy. There she was half altered and half the same. Candy. Candy was alive. Tears came.

François Vase coughed.

"As a devotee of nineteenth- and twentieth-century American culture, I have always thought that an ancient video of that time—*The Wizard of OZ*—represents what really goes on in the successful harmonization of a mind implant. In a way it is like all good stories are implicitly. But the *Wizard of OZ* video is explicit. It's the story of a mixed-up person in Kansas coming to understand herself and her world better through living through the fantasy world of OZ.

"Only, of course"—François' eyes twinkled—"Kansas was a story too. As we—not just you—are all a story if we are to be understood. In order to tune mind and body you have to move them around. You can't correct a disharmony between eye and hand except by having eye watch while hand moves. To tune a mind and body you must have much of that stuff woven into personality and history. You need a story.

"We have here a story of Rim, of *Pequod,* of Houston. And if the Rim was just what we imagined, not the 'real' Rim—well, this Houston, this Norbert Wiener Research Hospital is just what we imagine it to be. The bare stuff of the place doesn't think. Reality is always unknowable, uh—"

The *uh* came when Candy goosed François. He did quite a commendable leap for someone his age. Candy perched on my bed. The familiar face was familiar on first sight. But somehow more vibrant. Her hands, those strong and capable hands, held mine. Her eyes glowed.

"You're here and we are here, Sally, that's what's important."

"Cat?" I said to her.

Germaine Means whistled.

"Cat's here too, or part of Cat," said Germaine.

A Vegan Siamese leaped on my bed next to Candy. The Siamese moved confidently up my body, planted forepaws on my breasts, and nuzzled my face. We somehow knew each other's movements.

"We used Koullah in the VAT for most of the cat part of the story," said Germaine in my ear.

"Zeet chizen, zeet chizen, sgood, sgood, Zally," said Koullah in her peculiar form of cat-English. Koullah grinned—if you can say that of a mentally augmented Vegan cat. Koullah looked like some sort of crazy miniaturization of the cat I had known.

"You mean you made me up," I said. I said it to Candy. "You made me up and none of it was real. I'm not real."

François Vase replied:

"No, Sally Forth—that is your name now, isn't it? —Candy and I, the rest of us, we didn't make you up, we didn't dream your dream. We tuned it.

"We didn't dream your dream any more than we constructed your muscles and motives. We posed a situation, we put people into your world, we got things together.

"But you determined what happened as much as we, Sally. And you made us as much as the reverse. Me especially."

Candy interrupted:

"What François means is that his VAT chamber was hooked with yours so that he felt every emotional or muscular reaction you came up with. Toned down a bit, of course. François' body couldn't take the physical strains you were taking."

I saw discolorations on Candy's shoulder. Like stinger scars, though much smaller.

"Yes, Sally, that too. Stigmata, you might call them. You got bruised and I got bruised. You can't tune a body without the physical end of it too. You could call the story fantasy but both of our bodies went through it."

"And," said Austin Worms, smiling down from behind Candy, "we had to replace the sensor pads in your VAT chamber six times. You *walked* a thousand kilometers even if you never left the VAT chamber. And you got alpha-level motor-muscular tone."

Germaine ran her fingers along Koullah's muzzle.

"Cat, too, you know," said Germaine. "We borrowed a cougar from the University of Houston. The mascot of the space-ball team. Koullah didn't have the right proportions for full contact. We figure you and the cougar got on well because you both had lots of weightlessness experience. You'll find you know something about maneuvering around big animals."

Then they showed me their instruments. The VAT operation theatre, its chambers and control modules, endless relays, transducers, data banks. On one wall, next to a facsimile of a first edition of Melville's *Moby Dick,* I saw a copy of the Dylan Thomas poem that Candy loved.

François Vase had explained to me how the harmonizers had started on the Moby Dick business. Sally Cadmus' ship had been called the *Baleen Blanco*

—the White Whale—which is what Moby Dick was. François and Candy had been unable to resist the sexual possibilities that this suggested.

On Germaine Means' master control module I saw a thick loose-leaf notebook. The label read *Ismael Forth + Sally Cadmus Logbook.* Germaine told me that I would be able to use the logbook if I wanted to write up my own account of my operation. Hence what you hold.

Afterwards we had a party in the lounge. We sang ghoul and vampire songs. And Austin Worms got quite drunk and sat next to me on a couch, alternating between kissing my cheek and crying, while François Vase, stretched out on the floor, rested his back on my legs. I declined his offer of heroin, though I did do some of Candy's Vegan leaf. I played with Koullah with my tail. Mind and body we.

At the end Germaine and Candy led me off to bed. Candy stayed. I saw her off at Houston Space Port the next day. There was something between us deeper than love.

Gxxhdt.

Etaoin shrdlu. Mmm.

Anti-M.

Away mooncow Taddy-fair fine. Fine again, take. Away, along, alas, alung the orbit-run, from swerve of space to wormhole wiggle, brings us. Start now. Wake.

So hear I

About the Author

JUSTIN LEIBER is at present a member of the Philosophy Department of the University of Houston, teaching courses about the mind/body problem, foundations of linguistics and psychology, and extraterrestrial communications. His free time is divided between writing, communing with cats, computers, and cougars, and wondering whether the electric ambiance of Houston represents the end of Western civilization or merely its transfiguration. He has a Ph.D. from the University of Chicago and a B. Phil. from Oxford University. His academic publications include *Noam Chomsky: A Philosophic Overview*, *Structuralism*, and many papers with intriguing titles, such as "Talking with Extraterrestrials," "Insulting," and "Paradigmatic Immorality." He has also taught at the City University of New York, Oxford University, and M.I.T. *Beyond Rejection* is his first novel and begins a trilogy.